The
L A S T
PRINCESS of
MANCHURIA

The
LAST
PRINCESS of
MANCHURIA

LILIAN LEE

Translated by Andrea Kelly

William Morrow and Company, Inc.
New York

This novel is a dramatization. Some of the facts have been embellished or exaggerated for dramatic effect, others have been left out, while still other "facts" are pure invention— this is a work of fiction, not history.

Library of Congress Cataloging-in-Publication Data

Li, Pi-hua.
    [Ch' uan-tao Fang-tzu. English]
    The last princess of Manchuria / Lilian Lee : translated by Andrea Kelly.
        p.   cm.
    Translation of: Ch' uan-tao Fang-tzu.
    ISBN 0-688-10834-2
    1. Kawashima, Yoshiko, 1906?-1948—Fiction.   I. Title.
PL2877.P48C44   1992
895.1'352—dc20   91-40506
                                                    CIP

Printed in the United States of America

First Edition

1 2 3 4 5 6 7 8 9 10

For Chris and Oona
—A. K.

I would like to thank all of those
people who were kind enough to speak to me
when I was researching this book.
They provided me with valuable
information—both official and
off the record.

The
LAST
PRINCESS of
MANCHURIA

Prologue

P eking. Late autumn.

Ten muscular strangers appeared at the main gate of number 34, Tung-ssu Lane Nine, in the district of Pei Chih-tzu.

All around was deathly silence. Even the men's breathing was soundless.

The autumn wind blew sadly, insistently.

Every trace of summer had long since vanished. Gone were the clamoring cicadas. Gone, too, were the Japanese invaders. They had all been scattered to the winds. Nothing remained— only the ghosts of the dead season's crickets, singing their mournful songs beneath the steps.

In the dark night, the grand old mansion appeared all the

more vast and imposing. It was like a dense forest, with its red pillars and doors and blue and green painted eaves. The past lay over the mansion like a heavy cloak, cutting it off from the outside world. Those who lived within its walls were sealed in a suffocating isolation.

A high threshold supported two massive doors. These were painted red and fitted with golden rings. One of the men knocked on the door.

They waited a long time. Finally, someone came. The door opened only a crack, but the men pushed their way in without a sound, pinning the old servant against the wall. Two of the men quickly chloroformed a pair of sleeping wolfhounds. Within moments, the "visitors" had the situation well in hand.

The old servant could only gape, wide-eyed, not daring to make a sound. All at once, his legs gave way underneath him, and he collapsed to his knees.

There were three entrances to the house. The ten-man squad hurried to the garden in back. Hearing the swift clip of fleeing footsteps, two of the men went off quickly in pursuit. No sooner had they raised their pistols than the man, a Japanese, surrendered, his head hanging dejectedly.

One of the big men asked with his eyes, Where is she?

The old servant silently led them to the back entrance and pointed to a room on the left. They all understood—the woman they had come for was inside.

The members of this "Special Operations Team" were well aware of the dangers and difficulties of their mission. When they received their high-level orders, they had gone to work right away. They set up thorough surveillance and carefully laid their plans. They had learned all that there was to know about their quarry; by now each knew her as well as he knew the palm of his own hand.

They were all hungry for this task. Was it because of the mystery and legend that lay at its center?

They had reached the final juncture. What if, at the last moment, something completely unexpected were to happen? What if they were to fail, just within sight of their goal? The men were confident in their training and abilities. Yet they were suddenly hit by a burst of uncertainty.

A wind bearing the hint of impending rain from the hills blew through the building.

One of the men gently pushed open the door to the room. Inside, everything was pitch-black.

They traded glances. Then, as swift as lightning, four of them rushed to the corners of the room. In the feeble light that came from outside, they could barely make out, in the center of the room, an unusually large brass bed. A canopy of mosquito netting spilled down around it. The canopy was topped with red silk gauze and hung from golden hooks. There were vague and shadowy outlines on the bed.

Was she on the bed?

Was that her?

They had heard so many stories about her—her exploits had shocked China and Japan. She was as beautiful and charming as an angel, but as cruel and poisonous as a witch. The men gripped their pistols tightly and broke into a cold sweat.

Their leader stepped forward softly and parted the netting, while behind him one of the others flicked on the light switch.

Suddenly, something round and fuzzy came hurtling out from behind the canopy, screeching loudly.

The men had been so tense that they all gave a start. There was the crack of a gunshot.

As the sound of the shot faded away, the furry thing bared its teeth in a miserable grimace and made an odd squealing noise.

Lying there in a pool of blood was a little monkey. It twitched violently as it died. With half-open, almost human eyes, it glared at the uninvited guests.

There was a slight shaking motion behind the netting. A woman cried out in shock:

"Ah-fu!"

She had called out as if she were dreaming. It had all been very quick, and the woman wasn't fully awake yet. The light pierced her tightly shut eyes. Half rising from the bed, she rubbed her eyes with a hand.

"Who the hell are you?" she demanded. "What are you doing here?"

The canopy parted a crack. A strange odor came welling out from the narrow opening. It was like a breath of poison, or the stench of an animal nursing a wound. It wasn't a human odor. Both rotten and raw, it was the smell of despair.

The men all fought back the urge to vomit. Gathering their wits, they waited for their "hostess" to make her entrance.

The first thing she presented was a hand. It had long, thin fingers and knobby bones. Through long neglect, it had taken on the greenish-yellow cast of a bird's claw. The crack in the gauze was opened a little wider, and half a face appeared.

The face belonged to a woman in her forties.

Thin and bony as kindling, with high cheekbones and short, unkempt hair, she looked haggard. She reminded them of a withered and crumpled flower. Had they found the wrong woman?

All the men looked stunned. For a moment, they were completely at a loss.

Was this really her?

The leader of the "Special Operations Team" ventured uncertainly, "You are . . . ?"

"Who are you looking for?" she countered.

The leader glanced at one of his comrades, and the other three quietly withdrew. The one the leader had singled out came forward, pointed a pistol at the woman, and ordered:

"Turn around, and take off your clothes!"

The woman looked up. It was then that she saw that this "man" was in fact a woman. Raising her head, she peered intently at this other woman.

She knew what this was for. Even if they didn't know her by her face, there was a feature on her body that she couldn't get rid of or hide. Her opponents had been thorough—in every way prepared to take her on. They even knew about the tiny red mole on her left breast!

To think that they had the gall to send a woman disguised as a man! Ha! What were they trying to prove? Putting on this pathetic show for *her* benefit?

Take off her clothes? Never!

She had always had a clear purpose in mind when she bared her flesh. She had always had her reasons. Her petite, exquisite body; her graceful, enticing breasts, with that one minute red spot, like a teardrop the color of blood—it had such an inutterable power to fascinate. Men's admiring tongues had teased at it, tickling her. In the past.

She wasn't about to bare herself only to be humiliated.

There was no escaping, anyway. If she was to make the best of an awkward position, there was no point in dwelling on the

past. She gritted her teeth, but it was the eyes in her tired and defeated face that gave the clearest account of her. Infinite dignity seemed to spring from them.

"There is no need for further discussion," she said. "I am Commander Chin Pi-hui, Yoshiko Kawashima!"

A black cloth sack was slipped over her proud head.

All she saw was blackness.

I

Yoshiko Kawashima had once wielded great power; but those glorious days were just memories now. In her heyday, she had cut quite a figure. She had strutted proudly in the crisp uniform and leather boots of a military officer. She had dressed herself in brocade dresses and thick fur coats. But all of that was gone. At the time of her arrest, she was wearing nothing but a very thin, faded blue nightshirt.

After the Japanese surrender, everything she owned had been confiscated, piece by piece. She could not believe that her protectors had been defeated until September of 1945, when she heard the Japanese emperor, Hirohito, declare the surrender. He had never spoken to his people before. With millions of others, she had listened to his dispirited announcement over the short-wave radio. It was then that she had realized that her days were numbered. Her sun had set.

She had immediately thrown all of her important papers into the fire. One of the few things that she spared from the flames was a finely wrought jewelry box. Its contents were priceless. Every piece of jewelry inside it was dazzlingly beautiful. There were pearls, diamonds, agates, jade, amber, other precious stones, all magnificent. She took out one of the necklaces and held it under the lamp. It was shaped like a phoenix and set with some thousand diamonds that sparkled and danced in the lamplight. The wings seemed to quiver as though the phoenix were about to take flight.

She also saved a photograph of herself, one that had formerly graced the front page of the newspaper. The photo showed a young woman with startlingly white skin and penetrating yet alluring eyes. She had been very beautiful. She had signed and dated this photo, as was her habit. Her writing was small and precise, with each character finely formed. The neat, controlled writing bore little resemblance to the woman who had written it. The inscription read:

Yoshiko Kawashima, 1934.

1934. The twenty-third year of the new Republic of China. Her beauty and powers had been at their peak, and the phoenix necklace she wore in the photo had been a perfect complement to her cheongsam, the traditional Chinese dress. The nation of Manchukuo had just been founded in Manchuria, her homeland, and she had been a part of it all.

Now, once again, this picture would appear on the front page of the paper; but this time it was not such a glorious occasion for her.

* * *

In an old neighborhood of Peking, a paperboy was carting around a huge stack of special-edition newspapers.

"Extra! Extra! Read all about it!" he yelled over and over, at the top of his lungs. "Traitor on trial! Yoshiko Kawashima on trial tomorrow!"

The front page article announced that the High Court of Hopei Province was set to open Yoshiko Kawashima's trial on the following day. There was also a list of the charges against her. Altogether, there were eight separate counts in the indictment; but they all amounted to the same thing: treason.

The paperboy was very young. Carried on his shrill and excited cries, the news penetrated every lane and alley of the neighborhood. As he made his rounds, he trampled a Japanese flag that had been thrown to the ground. Those who saw this felt their anger toward their old enemy reignited. Several passersby went out of their way to spit on this fallen symbol. It seemed as though their hatred for their former invaders would never be quenched.

A half-crazy middle-aged man came hobbling up. He was missing a leg and an eye, and he stumbled straight into the boy. Seeing what a pathetic state this old veteran was in, nobody could be angry with him.

"Peace has come! We've won! We really sent those Japanese devils packing!" The madman laughed with bizarre delight.

Schoolchildren had been given the day off, and everybody turned out to watch the parades. They lined the streets, waving little Chinese flags emblazoned with a white sun on a field of deep blue sky. Strings of firecrackers went off all around, and scraps of paper from the exploded fireworks lay thickly on the ground. A pile of these tatters had drifted over a discarded copy of the special-edition newspaper, burying Yoshiko's beautiful face.

Yoshiko had been abandoned by her former protectors. She had become like the rest of the useless articles the Japanese had left behind in their flight. Kimonos, fans, jewelry boxes, fancy brocade sandals, and the elaborate wigs so popular with young Japanese women at the turn of the century were all that remained of the occupation. From Tung Tan to Pei Hsin-chiao, streetside stalls were piled high with such things. The vendors were selling them off at cut-rate prices, trying to get rid of them as fast as they could. Thus was marked the passing of an era.

Chinese and American soldiers and steel-helmeted Chinese military police now stood where the bullying Japanese military police had once held sway. The day that the long-suffering people of China had yearned for had finally arrived. They had been liberated from a cruel occupation. They could enjoy a brief respite; although in truth their trials were far from over.

In the lull that followed Japan's defeat, the sensational "Traitor's Trial" brought an air of festivity to China's capital. It had been a year since her arrest, and the people of Peking looked forward to the trial with eager anticipation, as though it were a festival like the Chinese New Year. At the same time, they had been under the Japanese boot for so long that they were still filled with hatred and anger. Anti-Japanese sentiments still ran high, and former collaborators were often savagely pelted with bricks and stones by irate citizens.

Everybody was talking about Yoshiko:

"I hear she's a real looker!"

"Sure, but she also murdered lots of Chinese people!"

"She's just a woman—and such a tiny thing, too. How could she possibly be as tough as they say?"

"Let's get some more bricks!"

"Down with traitors and collaborators!"

The people's pent-up anger suddenly boiled over. But then, in the next instant, they were all whooping with joy. There, at the street corner, they had caught sight of a group of men doing the lion dance. It was just like a New Year's Day parade!

The war was over, but life in Peking still hadn't settled down. Not a day went by without some disruption or civil unrest. Prices were soaring. Paper money was worthless. And as for the newly printed Nationalist currency, well, nobody in his right mind had any faith in that! The only thing that had any value anymore was silver dollars.

Everybody had to struggle to keep afloat. And, as if their financial worries weren't bad enough, people kept hearing disturbing rumors that the Communists were about to march on Peking. The city was on edge.

So why shouldn't the public indulge in a little rowdy diversion? The spectacle of a spy trial was the perfect escape.

At 2:00 P.M. on the appointed day, some five thousand spectators crowded into the rear courtyard of the courthouse, which had been transformed into a temporary observation gallery. They had pushed their way in, hoping to catch a glimpse of the star of the show, the infamous Yoshiko Kawashima. The authorities were unable to maintain order, and everything in the courtyard was trampled, while many windows were smashed.

The authorities had arranged this drama with the intention of making it a cautionary tale. They were to make an example of the defendant, an example that would awe the public into submission. But the plan backfired, as the excited crowd quickly got out of control. Amid much commotion and scuffling in the audience, a recess was announced. The court had been in session for less than thirty minutes.

The din grew into an even louder uproar as the crowd roared its disappointment. They had come all this way just to get a peek at the beautiful and notorious Yoshiko. But now they were being packed off, and the great doors of the courthouse were being shut in their faces. Some hurled bricks at the courthouse out of frustration before quickly running away.

Eventually, the crowd broke up and everybody went home. Everybody, that is, but the star of the show. She was escorted to her new "home"—Municipal Prison Number One.

Three days later, the trial officially began.

On the first day, Yoshiko Kawashima appeared in court wearing a white sweater and green Western-style trousers. Her short hair was combed, but she was as thin and bony as she had been at her arrest. She had spent an agonizingly long year in custody, being carted from detention center to detention center. Now, at last, she had been brought to the defendant's box.

The magistrate gravely read out the charges against her:

"You are charged with the crime of treason against China. More specifically, you are charged with having aided and abetted Japan on Chinese soil, having collaborated with Japan, and having betrayed the interests of your native land. These are all treasonable acts of the basest sort.

"If you are found guilty of the crime of treason, you shall be punished either by death or by life imprisonment, in accordance with the punishments set down by the legislature."

Yoshiko listened to the magistrate's pronouncements with a dismissive air. Really, he hardly merited her attention at all. She waited until he had finished reading the charges. Then, without warning, she poked her face right into his. He was visibly startled.

"Your Honor," she said coolly, "may I have a cigarette?"

The judge nodded his assent, and the bailiff handed her a cigarette. Yoshiko placed it in her mouth and fixed her eye on the judge, waiting. Somewhat reluctantly, he gave her a light.

Yoshiko haughtily took a long pull on the cigarette. She languidly exhaled a cloud of pale smoke, waiting for the magistrate to begin his attack.

He held up a book. Printed in large characters on the cover was the title, *Venus in a Suit*. The author's name, Shofu Muramatsu, was Japanese.

"Are you familiar with this novel?" the magistrate asked.

"Yes," she replied blandly.

"Are you also familiar with the author of this book?"

"Well, I've seen his name in the papers. He's a fairly well known Japanese novelist, isn't he?"

The judge struggled to keep his temper in check. She was toying with him.

"This novel contains information," the judge said tensely, "furnished personally, by you, to the author—information concerning your treasonous collaboration with the Japanese and your scheming with them to set up an independent state in Manchuria and Mongolia."

"Come now, Your Honor," she said lazily. "You yourself just characterized this as a novel, a work of fiction! Have you ever read any of China's classic novels, like *Journey to the West* or *The Golden Lotus?* They're as full of the same scandalous and shocking things—the same seductions and temptresses—as the so-called 'evidence' you're presenting here. I don't suppose you're planning to drag all of these other fictional malfeasants into court as well?"

The courtroom erupted in raucous laughter.

"The court expects the defendant to treat these proceedings

with appropriate respect and seriousness," the magistrate admonished her angrily. "Remember that you are addressing a court of law."

Yoshiko immediately assumed a serious manner.

"I address others as they address me—and as befits them. I would expect the court to find a more serious and credible individual to question me," she said, superciliously taking another drag on her cigarette.

Suppressing his anger, the magistrate changed tack.

"As for the secretary who was arrested along with you at your house in Pei Chih-tzu, one Hachiro Ogata—"

Yoshiko cut him off.

"Mr. Ogata is a secretary in name only," she responded swiftly in Ogata's defense. "He is a good man, and a faithful servant. He knows absolutely nothing, and he is innocent of any wrongdoing! You had no business arresting him! I, and I alone, am accountable for my actions. Keep him out of it!"

"All right, then. We won't discuss him. Let's talk about some other people instead, shall we? For instance, Naniwa Kawashima. Mitsuru Kashirayama. Yosuke Matsuoka. Daisaku Komoto. Fumimaru Konoe. Hideki Tojo. Shigeru Honjo. Kenji Tohibara. Shunkichi Uno. Hanji Ito. Seishiro Itagaki."

Yoshiko listened calmly as the judge recited this string of names. Men's names, all of them. And all of them Japanese men. She'd spent half of her life under the thumbs of these Japanese men, being passed from one to another. And what for? Was it only so that she could be brought to this humiliating defeat?

No!

When she spoke again, it was without hurry. She formed each word clearly and one at a time.

"I have not betrayed China. I am not a Chinese traitor."

She shot a glance at the magistrate to gauge his reaction before she continued in the same clear voice.

"I am Japanese! I am not Chinese!"

The courtroom was in an uproar. She wouldn't even admit that she was Chinese! The nerve!

At the heart of this incredible and shocking claim there may have been a grain of truth. Had she turned her back on China; or had China rejected her first?

She had only been seven years old when she was sent away.

2

She was a seven-year-old girl with white ribbons in her hair. Her mother was trying desperately to coax her into letting the servants dress her in a white kimono.

"I am Chinese!" Hsien-tzu Aisin-Gioro shrieked tearfully, struggling to free herself from the strange, foreign garment. "I am not Japanese!"

She was just a child, naive in the ways of the world, and she could not possibly have imagined what fate had in store for her. Perhaps it was some instinctive sense of the significance of what was happening to her that made her resist. Despite her age, she already had a strong will. And at this moment, the full force of that will was bent on one thing: not putting on the white silk kimono.

Her mother, the fourth ancillary concubine of Prince Su of the Ching royal family, was the youngest and most beautiful of the prince's many consorts. Prince Su doted to the point of worship on this elegant twenty-nine-year-old with long, luxuriant hair. It was hardly surprising that her daughter—Hsien-tzu, the fourteenth child out of twenty-one little princes and seventeen little princesses—should also be one of his favorites. At this particular moment, however, she did not feel particularly favored. She stood there with tears streaming down her face and cried out in her shrill child's voice:

"I don't want to go to Japan!"

"Be a good girl, and don't cry," her mother entreated.

Hsien-tzu's mother then took her by the hand and led the child to Prince Su's study. She brought her right up to the prince, who was sitting at his desk.

The little girl was in complete awe of her father, and more than a little bit afraid of him, too. Even in ordinary clothes he had a princely air, with his formal manners and serious expression. He was quite an intimidating man, and Hsien-tzu and her brothers and sisters always did their best to steer clear of him. But now here she was, face-to-face with him! She wasn't used to being this close, and it made her very uncomfortable.

The prince and his family were all members of the Ching imperial family, but this did not carry as much weight as it used to. The once-mighty Ching dynasty had been destroyed and replaced by the Chinese Republic in 1911.

The last Ching emperor, Pu-yi, had been forced out of power by General Yuan Shih-kai, and the royal family had fled Peking, scattering to other parts of the country. Some of these nobles had chosen to live in peaceful retirement. Others, like Prince Su, had bided their time, awaiting an opportunity to restore the Ching dynasty.

Prince Su had never been fooled by the ambitious General Yuan. Yuan did not want democracy, as he so often claimed. He wanted to be emperor himself! And besides, as far as Prince Su was concerned, Yuan was fundamentally untrustworthy: He was Chinese. Like all of the Ching royal family, Prince Su was not ethnically Chinese but Manchu, a descendant of the nomadic tribes that originally roamed the northeastern corner of the Chinese Empire. Prince Su did not trust the Chinese on principle. While Yuan was consolidating his power, the prince threw in his lot with the Japanese, and one Japanese fellow in particular: Naniwa Kawashima.

Kawashima was a Japanese adventurer who had first come to the prince's attention back in 1900 during the Boxer Rebellion. The Forbidden City had been surrounded by foreign troops, and Kawashima had presented himself at the palace gates. There, with his flawless Chinese, Kawashima had persuaded the palace guards not to resist. He pointed out to them that stubborn resistance could only result in the senseless destruction of the proud and splendid Forbidden City. Artillery fire would damage its magnificent halls; and looting would strip it of its treasures. Surely, they did not want that! Convinced by his smooth arguments, the guards surrendered.

After this incident, Prince Su and Kawashima became fast friends. The two would spend hours sitting around the fire together, laughing at the follies of current politics. They found that they had much in common. They had similar tastes and temperaments, and they shared the same dream. Both believed fervently in the future of the Ching dynasty. As long as there was a China, they agreed, the great Ching Empire would never perish!

As the dynasty limped along in its final days, Prince Su was the only member of the Ching imperial family who refused to give up trying to resuscitate it and restore it to its former glory.

He planned to go to Mukden, in Manchuria, to join the local warlord Chang Tso-lin, who was raising an army to take on General Yuan's forces. But only ten days after Prince Su left the capital, Emperor Pu-yi formally turned over all political powers to the provisional Nationalist government. This was tantamount to abdication.

Prince Su was left with no alternative but to flee to Port Arthur, on the Manchurian coast, where he took refuge in the Japanese concession. It was there that he began to devise an even grander scheme. His fourteenth daughter, Princess Hsien-tzu, was a part of his plan. No, she was not merely part of the plan—she was the key to the entire thing!

The prince's Port Arthur residence was an immense, Russian-style red brick mansion set high on a ridge in dense woods. It had altogether twenty-eight rooms. Prince Su's study was on the second floor.

"Come, pay your respects to your father and wish him farewell," Hsien-tzu's mother instructed her.

Timidly, the little girl raised her tear-streaked face.

Her father, this all-powerful head of their household of a hundred people, sat before her, regarding her gravely. He was the tenth bearer of the hereditary title Prince Su. If the Ching dynasty had still held sway, his family would have been the leader of the eight hereditary clans of the Manchu nobility. The prince possessed both a strong character and a natural air of authority. He was a farsighted planner and a capable leader, as well. His demand for order extended even to the most commonplace of domestic rituals, such as family meals. At mealtimes, everybody waited obediently for the sound of the gong before assembling in the mansion's huge dining room.

Hsien-tzu usually watched him from some inconspicuous

corner. But now he was very close, right in front of her. He looked intently at his seven-year-old daughter.

"Hm . . . Yes, my Hsien-tzu looks most gallant in her kimono—just as I knew she would."

For a moment, he seemed lost in thought.

"From this day forward," he continued, "I shall call you Tung-chen—Eastern Jewel. I hope that when you have gone east to Japan, you will be an honored and treasured guest."

Having no idea what he meant, Hsien-tzu merely nodded.

"Tung-chen," Prince Su said. "Do you know why I have chosen to send you? Because, of all my sons and daughters, you are by far the most promising. I am counting on you—you and Mr. Kawashima!"

All the objects in the study were lit up by the brilliant light of a French ceiling lamp. There was a sofa, upholstered in scarlet velvet. There were bookcases, too, filled with copies of ancient Chinese classics, reference works, manuscripts, and various documents. These gave off the pleasant odor of paper and ink. There were other treasures here, as well. Her father even had a large glossy photo of the famous Peking opera star Mei Lan-fang, in performance. Yet out of this room full of marvelous things, all that her father gave her was a rather dingy snapshot, gray-spotted and odd-looking.

It was a picture of Naniwa Kawashima. This was the Japanese adventurer in whom the prince had placed his faith, the man who had devised an ambitious plan for the creation of an independent Manchuria and Mongolia. To this end, he had assiduously studied Manchuria, and his knowledge of the region was encyclopedic. Indeed, he knew far more about Manchuria than most Chinese people did.

The man looked out from the picture with penetrating eyes

that were shadowed by heavy eyebrows. He was rather gaunt and had a learned air. He sat stiff and erect in his kimono, gazing into the distance with a pleased smile.

"This is your foster father," Prince Su told his daughter. "He will prepare you well for your role in a great undertaking: You are to participate in the restoration of the Ching dynasty. This man will guide you. You must obey him."

Kawashima had made personal sacrifices for the Ching cause. His devotion had gone beyond his friendship with Prince Su. He had gone so far as to grow his hair long so that he could wear a Manchu braid. He had also become an avid student of Chinese history and geography. Although his youthful plans for an independent Manchuria and Mongolia had been crushed, he had never given up hope. He held fast to his belief that the territory of Manchuria was the key to Japan's future survival.

Manchuria was quite a prize. This splendid land that occupied the northeastern corner of China was rich in natural resources as well as being strategically located.

Although he was actually a year older than Prince Su, Kawashima had cleverly told the prince that they had been born in the same year. In a further show of flattery, he took to respectfully addressing the prince as his elder, and the two quickly became fast friends. They had even become adopted brothers, exchanging horoscopes as part of the ritual. It was on that day that Kawashima, dressed in the robes of a Ching official, had posed for a commemorative photograph with Prince Su. They were seated side by side, in front of a Japanese wisteria screen.

Prince Su handed his daughter a letter, instructing her to deliver it to Kawashima. The message read:

I give you this little trinket. I hope that you will always treasure her.

Hsien-tzu's carriage arrived, and the entire household came out to see off the sweet-faced but teary-eyed "little trinket."

The garden of the prince's residence was ablaze with flowers as brilliant and multicolored as silk brocade. There were peach trees, apricot trees, acacias, sunflowers, and eight kinds of cherries, all in bloom. It was spring of the year 1913. Seven-year-old Hsien-tzu, still an innocent, was setting out for Japan all alone.

3

When Hsien-tzu, now also called Tung-chen, disembarked at Shimonoseki, the man in the picture was there to meet her, as promised. His heavy eyebrows were knit tightly together, as though serious troubles were weighing on his mind.

The child had never seen this man before, and she had no feelings for him at all. Yet he was to be her "father," and she went with him, home to the Akabane district of Tokyo.

He, too, gave her a new name, a Japanese name: Yoshiko Kawashima. Yoshiko would learn to sign her name in Japanese, speak Japanese, and sip miso soup, just like a little Japanese girl.

Naniwa Kawashima had looked worried that first day, because the political situation in China was changing rapidly. Indeed, by January of 1915, things would have changed so drastically that Kawashima would be forced to alter his plans completely. For it was then, just as Kawashima was actively promoting Ching restoration, that Japan had confronted China with the so-called "Twenty-one Demands." Had China agreed to all of them, it would have become, in effect, a Japanese protectorate. The attitude of the Japanese government was completely inflexible, and the demands were so outrageous that not only did the people of China reject them as preposterous, there was even a segment of Japanese society that criticized these demands. Nonetheless, Chinese president Yuan Shih-kai agreed to most of the conditions, with disastrous results for China. Turning his back on the people of China, Yuan donned the dragon robes of a Chinese emperor and strutted about the political stage, calling himself emperor. But before people even had time to catch their breath, this "emperor" was dragged from the stage. The people waited for the next act in this spectacle.

Naniwa Kawashima's original plan had been to unite Inner and Outer Mongolia with the three provinces of Manchuria: Mukden, Kirin, and Heilungchiang. Here he would install the deposed Ching emperor, Pu-yi, as sovereign. This enterprise required money, able strategists, and troops.

As a primary-school student, Yoshiko Kawashima did not receive any of the moral guidance a child normally should. Instead, everything she learned outside of her regular schoolwork was geared to foster in her an intense love and longing for her "Manchurian homeland." She was completely innocent of the true purpose underlying her education. Even if she had known, she probably would not have been able to understand.

Kawashima kept Yoshiko close to him, and the only time

she ever got to play with her classmates was during recess in the schoolyard. The boys all had shaved heads, and they looked like mass-produced toy soldiers lined up in their uniforms of cotton jackets and twill pants. All the little girls wore printed silk jackets and purple satin culottes.

Physical education at this school included military drills, which, for the boys, included sparring with bamboo sticks. The object of this game was to conquer China. If you could "penetrate" China, then you could eat fresh sweet pears, live in a fancy house, and be waited on by Chinese servants. And everybody knew that Chinese servants were the most loyal and obedient in the whole world.

During recess the children also liked to play fighter planes. One day Yoshiko was the fighter plane. She flew around, bombing her classmates, and one by one they all fell down. But one little boy refused to fall down. Yoshiko charged ahead, humming like an engine and making exploding noises, and she pushed him roughly to the ground.

When the boy hit the ground, he started to cry.

"What are you crying about?" Yoshiko taunted him. "If there's a war, you'll be the first to die, you chicken!"

"Hey, Yoshiko," another child asked slyly. "Where are you from, anyway?"

"China? Japan? Where?" another chimed in.

Yoshiko was tongue-tied. The truth was, she wasn't sure what country she was from. She was all mixed up, and the confusion threw her off balance.

On inspiration, she cleverly replied, "I'm from my mother's stomach!"

Then she turned on her heel and sped away. She ran and ran; but where was she running? No matter how fast or far she ran, she was still in a foreign country. This wasn't her home, and it never could be. She tried to recall her home; but try as she might, she couldn't even remember her mother's face.

Unbidden, tears began to fill her eyes, but she didn't feel sad, exactly. It was more of a vague and lonely emptiness.

A rubber ball came flying over from the distant playing field and landed at her feet. A little boy came running after the ball, but before he was able to retrieve it, Yoshiko quickly snatched it up. Using every ounce of her strength, she nastily threw it even farther away. This was the hard side of her personality, seen only in flashes now; but as the years went by, it would show itself more frequently, and with more intensity.

She ran on, home to her foster father, Kawashima, while all the time her classmates called mockingly after her:

"Yoshiko! Yoshiko! Little Chinese Yoshiko!"

Yoshiko didn't want to go back to school. The group-oriented regimentation of school life went completely against her nature. She switched schools countless times and went through a number of private tutors, but she was never satisfied. The only thing that remained constant was that Kawashima set her daily lessons. Day and night, he saw to it that she was inculcated with thoughts of Ching restoration and an independent Manchuria. In this way, step by step, Yoshiko grew up.

A thousand miles away in China, life went on. In 1916, President Yuan Shih-kai died in somewhat mysterious circumstances. Some said he had died of illness; others said it was a cerebral hemorrhage triggered by shock; and still others said he had been assassinated. But in the end it didn't really matter to Kawashima and Prince Su. They had been mustering their forces to mount an operation that would have brought down Yuan and restored the Ching. With Yuan's death, they suddenly found themselves without an objective. It was as though somebody had stuck a pin into an overinflated balloon. Prince Su was despondent and slid into a depression.

The following year, there was another failed attempt to restore the Ching dynasty. This time it started in the south. After only twelve days, it was soundly defeated; but in the aftermath of the affair, China's political situation was even more confused than before. Nothing had been settled, despite an official return to the Ching calendar.

Kawashima and Prince Su had another ally, a Mongolian general named Babujab. He fought long and hard to realize their goals, but he met with political failure and a violent death. After several years of scattered skirmishes, Prince Su and Kawashima's money and ammunition were all spent. They had squandered their resources and achieved nothing. Discouraged as Kawashima was by these many setbacks, he still had a card up his sleeve.

Yoshiko was now almost fifteen. This evening she was sitting by the window of their new house and gazing up at the starry sky. They had left Tokyo and taken lodgings near the Asama Hot Springs in Shinshu.

The stars in the sky came in many colors. There were yellow ones, blue ones, silver ones, and red ones. They were like multicolored spangles sewn onto a black sash of night sky. Yoshiko sat there, just gazing at the stars, for a very long time.

Gradually, a sense of desolation crept over her. She began to feel uneasy, but all she had to do was remember her mission, and she cheered up immediately. The mighty Ching dynasty will always have me! My homeland needs me, and I won't let it down! she thought to herself. Encouraged by these thoughts, she was filled with passion and a renewed sense of purpose. Kawashima's years of painstaking training had been well spent on this young woman. Yoshiko had by now become a shrewd and fearless young girl; and, although she was impulsive, she had guts and the ability to think for herself.

Yoshiko had transferred midyear to Matsumoto Girls High School. Her attendance and scholarship were poor at best. She went to class only when she was in the mood. When she got bored, she simply slipped away. Neither threats nor cajolery could persuade her to change her ways.

She had just sneaked out of class one day when Kawashima appeared at the school. She was passing the time of day with the school handyman, chatting and laughing merrily.

"Yoshiko!" her foster father called to her.

One look at the serious expression on his face told her that something was wrong. He put an arm around her thin shoulders. Although she was rather slight, her muscles were strong and firm.

"Yoshiko," he said gravely. "I have more bad news for you. You must be strong. It's your father. He passed away on the twenty-seventh, in Port Arthur—diabetes."

Kawashima's words filled Yoshiko's mind. More bad news, she thought. Only a month before, news of her mother's death had reached them. People said that her mother had been pregnant with her eleventh child. Wanting to devote all of her attention to looking after Prince Su, she had decided not to have the child. She had taken what she thought was a mild dose of poison to induce a miscarriage; but she had miscalculated the dosage and had accidentally killed herself.

Now Yoshiko's father was gone, too.

It was as though all of her family ties had been severed. She was completely on her own, alone in the world.

"Don't be sad, Yoshiko," Kawashima was admonishing her.

"Remember, we must carry on with your father's work. We must restore the Ching dynasty!"

Yoshiko said nothing. She had just received a great blow, yet she betrayed no emotion. Dry-eyed, she set her jaw, her face as cold and unmoving as jade.

Her unshakable composure was the result of Kawashima's strict upbringing. Yoshiko bore little resemblance to the "little trinket" who had been so prone to tears and tantrums. She had grown into a strong young woman who never shed tears. Her foster father regarded her solemnly.

"We are all waiting for you to grow up," he said.

Indeed, their work was still unfinished. Her father's grand dreams were still unfulfilled. Kawashima's ambitious schemes were still just extravagant talk. Yoshiko was to be the final gambit, but she was not yet ready to be played. She was like a blossom that had yet to burst into bloom, a thoroughbred that had never been run.

Through everything, and against many odds, Yoshiko had never forgotten who she was, and she never forgot her position in her family. She had grown up in a world torn by revolution and political upheaval, had been separated from her family at an early age to be raised in Japan by an ambitious stranger. Any feelings of attachment she might have had for her family had all but been destroyed in the intervening years. Nonetheless, she remembered who she was—the fourteenth daughter of Prince Su, and a Manchu princess—and she knew what was required of her. She rushed back to Peking to attend her father's funeral, as was her duty.

Prince Su's coffin was conducted from Port Arthur to Peking by a long cortege of pall-bearers, sutra chanters, mourners, and assistants carrying the paper replicas of money and other personal articles that the spirit of the deceased would need in the afterlife. The procession was so long that it took an entire day for it to travel from the gates of the prince's residence to the Port Arthur train station. The funeral rituals were second only to an emperor's in strictness and formality, and the pomp of the ceremony would have suited an emperor.

After her father's funeral, Yoshiko returned to school in Japan; but she had even less taste for academic work than before. She took any opportunity she could find to take days off. When she had been absent from class for some time, her headmaster lost patience and threatened to expel her. But Yoshiko did not care in the least. She had fallen in love.

4

Yoshiko's was a wild and playful young love. She would put on a sailor suit and cap and go out riding with her sweetheart. She looked almost like a boy, except that her long hair fell well past her shoulders, and it blew in the wind as she galloped along.

Her sweetheart's name was Toru Yamaga. He was a second lieutenant in the Fiftieth Infantry Company of Matsumoto, and a candidate for the military academy. Adventurer, patriot, and radical, he was also a member of the shadowy group known as the Black Dragon Society. This organization of nationalistic militarists had ties to Japanese military intelligence and was committed to the goal of establishing Japanese control over East Asia.

Its primary objective was Northeast China—Manchuria.

Men of all descriptions regularly came to Naniwa Kawa-shima's house to attend meetings and carry on loud and bombastic political discussions deep into the night. Yamaga had been one of them, but his interest was soon distracted from international affairs by the beautiful young Yoshiko. As the pair found them-selves inexorably drawn to one another, they became increasingly uninterested in politics.

Yoshiko was now seventeen years old, and she had devel-oped a unique kind of charm—an intriguing blend of femininity and aggressiveness. But she was still a child in many ways.

The young couple often went riding together. Yoshiko rode well, but Yamaga was far more accomplished. With a swift and subtle movement, he would urge his horse to spring into a gallop, leaving Yoshiko far behind. Then, with just a tug on the reins, Yamaga could make his horse stop and rear up on its hind legs, so that man and horse both stood tall and gallant.

He was a soldier, and he rode like one, with bravado. His horsemanship seemed to be one fancy, hair-raising maneuver after another. As he raced along, his body often rose far out of the saddle, so that he seemed to be flying through the air.

Yoshiko did not like to be outdone, and today these stunts of Yamaga's bothered her even more than usual. Of course, she adored him, but she hated his being so much more skillful than she was. Determined to keep up with him, she made her body light and let herself rise out of the saddle as she galloped. Sud-denly, she lost her balance and started to slip off the horse.

Yamaga saw that Yoshiko was about to take a fall. He quickly spun his horse around, rushed back to her, and lifted her lightly back into her saddle. Yoshiko gave him a grateful smile.

The two rode on companionably for the rest of the afternoon. It was only hours later that they realized how exhausted they were and turned for home.

When they reached Yoshiko's house, they found that Kawashima had company. Today, as on many days, the house near Asama Hot Springs was filled with distinguished guests. The entryway was lined with rows of the boots and shoes Kawashima's guests had removed upon entering the house. The walls were hung with hats and overcoats, and a variety of walking sticks filled the umbrella stand.

Who was inside Kawashima's meeting room and what they were conferring about were matters of complete indifference to Yoshiko. She could only stare at Yamaga—she looked right through the rest as if they weren't even there.

Yamaga accompanied his sweetheart as far as the entryway.

"I'll see you tomorrow," he said, barely able to stand even the thought of parting.

Yoshiko looked at him sternly.

"You may not leave yet!" she said, assuming a commanding tone of voice. Then she spun around swiftly and ran to the kitchen. Intent on her errand, she was oblivious to the babble of voices that came from behind Kawashima's study door as she passed by.

She soon returned to Yamaga, bearing a confection box. She opened the box, and Yamaga saw that it contained rice cakes. They were filled with sweetened *azuki* paste.

"I made these myself," Yoshiko said, picking up one of the cakes. She took a bite and passed it to him.

He scowled.

"Not *azuki* paste again!" he said with annoyance.

"I like it!"

"It's too sweet! I like chestnut filling."

Yoshiko shook her head but didn't say a word. She then took out the gob of rice cake she had been chewing and shoved it into his mouth, not taking her eyes off him until he had swallowed it all.

"I don't like chestnut filling," she said firmly. "But next time I promise to make some just for you—if you have eaten every cake in this box by tomorrow."

Yamaga glanced surreptitiously at the contents of the box. There were eight of them! And they were all several inches across! One look at Yoshiko told him he had better do as he was told, and he graciously took the box.

Yoshiko brimmed with satisfaction. Ever since childhood, she had been a little dictator. This autocratic streak was complimented by a well-developed talent for wheedling. One of her greatest pleasures was keeping her loved ones wrapped around her little finger.

"Next time," she said silkily, "I promise to use chestnut filling. And if I break my promise, I'll make it up to you by using only chestnut filling for the rest of my life!"

She gave him a sidelong glance. He was almost ten years her senior, but he was putty in her hands.

"I want to prove to you that I am a good woman."

Yamaga laughed and quickly drew himself to attention.

"You are the good woman of Second Lieutenant Yamaga of the Fiftieth Infantry Company of Matsumoto! My respects, miss!" he said, saluting her.

Yoshiko seemed to reflect on this for a moment.

"Matsumoto is such a tiny place. . . . Oh, never mind. Anyway, don't forget—you have to eat them all! You will be interrogated tomorrow!" Having said this, she turned to go inside; but after only a few steps, she looked back at him and admonished him sweetly:

"See you tomorrow!"

She watched him leap onto his horse and ride away, her eyes lingering lovingly on his receding form. He was like his horse—proud and strong—and he gave a lusty shout as he rode off.

A contented smile spread over her face. She could almost have forgotten all of her lofty ambitions. Let the others go racing off to China! They could go without her! All that she wanted in the world was to be with her love, to care for him, and to have him care for her. Together they could travel far and fly high. She was no different from other women, after all. She could find her happiness in loving a man.

"Yoshiko!"

She did not hear.

"Yoshiko!"

The call from inside the house came again, dragging her spirit back to the present.

The smile had not yet faded from her cheeks as she called out a response and made her way to the study. She slid open the wooden door.

All eyes in the room were on her, and she gave a start. There were about a dozen men gathered in the study, all dashing and brave idealists, filled with the spirit of adventure. There was something very unnerving about having a dozen men staring at her so intently. She felt oddly out of place: Once again, she had stumbled into the world of men.

Seated next to Naniwa Kawashima was a man with pure white hair and beard and a deceptively kind face. His name was Mitsuru Kashirayama, and he was the leader of the Black Dragon Society. He gave Yoshiko a thorough looking-over. With his air of quiet authority, he had a way of commanding attention without being threatening.

Mitsuru Kashirayama and Naniwa Kawashima saw eye to

eye when it came to the goal of realizing Japan's desire to conquer the Asian continent and the rationale behind it. In their view, the Chinese race had been completely corrupted by five thousand years of stagnant civilization. Chinese society had all but disintegrated, and its 400 million people were as scattered and aimless as windblown grains of sand. The Chinese people were selfish, egotistical, and shortsighted—they were enslaved by a dying nation.

The time had come for Japan to assert its natural superiority. With its superior strength, Japan would have little difficulty in establishing its first foothold in the Chinese territories of Manchuria and Mongolia. Having occupied this corner of the land, they could use it as a base from which to extend their influence throughout Asia, until they reached their ultimate goal: to become the masters of Asia. It was imperative that other world powers not be allowed to claw China apart, piece by piece. The Japanese were especially wary of Russia, which eyed China like a hungry beast.

When Yoshiko walked in on them, it was just these questions—and what to do about Manchuria and Mongolia, in particular—that Kawashima and his guests were discussing.

"I look forward to the day when the skies of Manchuria will be the roof over our heads, the earth of Manchuria will be our bed, and our names will be engraved upon China's five thousand years of troubled history!" Kawashima declaimed.

Yoshiko nodded her head in greeting to the assembled guests. To some extent, almost every one of the ambitious young men seated in Kawashima's study was a secret admirer of Yoshiko. Indeed, each may have dedicated his youth to something more than politics and the fate of the nation. Perhaps their political activism had become little more than a cover for another objective. After all, Yoshiko was just seventeen, beautiful, haughty, and a pure-blooded Manchu princess. And despite her breeding, she had a recklessness and unconventionality that made her all the more attractive. She would have been an appealing bride even without her political connections.

While most of the men in the room were watching her with admiration, there was one pair of eyes that watched her with a more intense longing. In a room full of competitors, all vying for her, could it be that the strongest contender was the one who said the least? Was his silence real . . . or contrived?

"Yoshiko," Kawashima said, "do you recognize this man?"

Her gaze rested on the silent young man's face. He returned her gaze, looking at her directly, without blinking. His eyes shone with vitality. He had said nothing, but she couldn't help liking him. She felt she had known him all her life.

"He is Ganjurjab, the second son of the Mongolian general Babujab."

Of course! It all came rushing back to her now. This was Prince Ganjurjab, her childhood playmate. And he hadn't changed a bit—he was just the way he had been as a little boy.

Yoshiko and Ganjurjab had been very close as children. Their two princely fathers had shared great plans, while the children had shared an innocent affection for each other. Later, they had gone their own separate ways. She had been sent away to be raised by Kawashima, while he had entered the Japanese Army's Officer Training School.

In spite of the fact that he had grown into a tall and handsome man, Yoshiko was unable to suppress a giggle. She was remembering how, one day, one of the grown-ups had taken a picture of them together. Just as the photographer was about to take the picture of the carefully posed children, Yoshiko had whispered mischievously in Ganjurjab's ear.

"Let's pretend we're playing Paper, Scissors, Stone—you make a fist and be 'stone,' and I'll be the 'scissors,' okay?"

Ganjurjab had always been a shy and timid child, and he didn't like to make mischief. So he pretended not to hear her. When the picture was developed, it showed a polite little Ganjurjab with his hands folded properly in his lap, next to Yoshiko with her "scissors."

No, he hadn't changed at all, from the look of him. She thought she detected a faint blush spreading across his face.

"Do you remember him?" Kawashima said again. "It's been a long time since you two have seen one another. Now, two old friends are meeting again. He has graduated from the military academy."

"Oh?"

Kawashima was trying to gauge Yoshiko's reaction. For her part, Yoshiko had a funny feeling that something was up, although she couldn't put her finger on it. What could it be? She felt a gnawing suspicion. There was something about this reunion that seemed too carefully orchestrated, too artificial. But Yoshiko quickly dismissed these uneasy feelings—she had something else on her mind, Yamaga.

The white-haired gentleman, Kashirayama, nonchalantly raised his cup and took a sip of sake.

5

The day of Yoshiko's reunion with Ganjurjab, October 6, 1924, was to be the turning point in Yoshiko's life. If history had passed over this day and missed it entirely, perhaps none of this would have happened, and Yoshiko's life never would have become the dazzling and terrible dream now recorded in history. But, then again, perhaps everything that followed was fate.

It all started simply enough. Yoshiko had just finished taking her evening bath when Kawashima called her into his study.

It was his custom to summon her when he had a new idea to discuss. She was always the first to hear. Tonight, maybe he wanted to fill her in on what he and his comrades had talked about during their meeting. This would doubtless be followed by solemn lectures about political action and reminders that the dedicated activist had to know his enemy as well as himself if he were to achieve victory.

Drying herself off, Yoshiko put on her *yukata* robe and knotted the sash.

When she got to the study, Kawashima had lit the small stove, and on it a kettle of water was boiling gently. He liked to toss grapefruit peels into the fire—they gave off a pungent and fruity aroma that filled the room as they burned.

Yoshiko was surprised when Kawashima didn't bring up the usual subject of national affairs.

"Yoshiko," he asked simply, "have you ever given any thought to the question of marriage?"

He had caught her off balance.

"No, I—"

"By the standards of your country, you're already a bit overdue."

"My country? You mean . . . ?"

"Why, China, of course."

Yoshiko felt a touch of apprehension.

"But—but I'm Japanese."

"You just want to marry a Japanese man!" Kawashima countered quickly.

For a moment, Yoshiko was speechless. She lacked his years, his long experience of crafty manipulation. She was no match for him. With a nervous flutter, she waved the suggestion aside.

"No. Of course I don't. Love and marriage are two completely separate matters."

Kawashima pressed her.

"Is it Yamaga?" he asked. "He's nothing but a second lieutenant, you know."

"A second lieutenant can rise to be a first lieutenant in no time at all!" she said, refusing to give in so easily. "And he can rise through the ranks—right on up to lieutenant general, and even commander in chief. Everybody has to start out as a second lieutenant!"

"Of course he can rise through the ranks." Kawashima smiled. "If it all goes smoothly and there aren't any hitches, he can do it in about forty years."

He was right, and Yoshiko knew it. She said nothing.

"You are the fourteenth princess of a great Ching imperial clan. You must do great things—and not indulge in childish fantasies. You must never forget your father's legacy! Never mind that you are a princess—your mission, and your destiny, is that of a prince!"

"What is my mission?"

He had been waiting for her to ask this very question, so that he could explain to her just how important she was to their plans. She was the very key to their success.

When he spoke again, his voice had taken on a commanding edge.

"Your mission is to marry the Mongolian prince Ganjurjab. This will unite the military forces of Manchuria and Mongolia. These forces will cross northern China and capture Peking. There you will found an independent kingdom and restore the Ching emperor. These are important tasks!"

Yoshiko was stunned. So that's how it was. Ganjurjab! That explained everything.

"You're talking about a 'political marriage,' aren't you?" she said, and bowed her head, deep in thought. Marry Ganjurjab?

She certainly didn't despise him. But then, she couldn't say she especially liked him, either. If Yamaga was an eight on a scale of ten, then Ganjurjab was a five. Passable. But marry him?

For a long time, she didn't speak. She had been completely unprepared for this. What could she say? She was at a loss.

Kawashima gave Yoshiko a searching look, trying in vain to see into this young woman's heart. What was she thinking?

She weighed the matter carefully, calculating its merits and demerits; but she couldn't come to a decision. On one side was her duty to her country. On the other side was her heart's desire. If she chose to marry Ganjurjab and go away with him to Mongolia, her life would never be the same. There would be no turning back. She was so young, and in love for the first time. What was she to do?

Kawashima's gaze didn't waver.

"Compared to politics," he said levelly, "marriage is a trivial thing."

But Yoshiko didn't hear him. She was still turning the matter over in her mind. She wasn't aware that the collar of her robe had slipped back, revealing a slender band of snow-white neck covered with almost invisible down. Where the *yukata*'s lapels overlapped, it barely covered the hollow at her collarbone. The hollow of her neck was like a shallow vessel, waiting to be filled. Her graceful and delicate body had only just begun to blossom. She was still rather slight, but the charms of her body could easily be imagined.

Watching this tender and inexperienced young girl, Kawashima suddenly felt a shock run through his body. His heart seemed to stop. He was already fifty-nine years old. Yoshiko was only seventeen. He had raised her as a daughter and done his best to foster in her his own staunch political convictions. While he felt that he had made her what she was, he realized that she did not necessarily enjoy being controlled like a puppet. Before long, this young phoenix might spread her brilliant, fiery wings and fly far away from him.

She still hesitated. She didn't want to rush into anything. Perhaps there was something she could give to her sweetheart as a keepsake. . . .

Kawashima eyed her like a hungry wolf. He could have eaten her whole then and there. In one bite!

"A woman's virginity," Kawashima said hoarsely, "is also a trivial thing."

At first, Yoshiko didn't understand what he was saying. It was unthinkable. Unimaginable!

Slowly, it dawned on her. Her own foster father! The man who had been her guardian, who had overseen every aspect of her education and upbringing. He had been above suspicion. But now, in an instant, he had stepped over the line. How could he be so coarse? She had never once imagined that she would have to protect herself from him!

Kawashima roughly tore open the bottom half of her robe. As she struggled to break away, he saw for a moment the most secret and hidden part of her. She spun around and tried to run away, but he was right behind her. He grabbed the skirt of her robe and lifted it up over her waist, twisting it into a knot.

There were pale lilac flowers on her underpants.

Her half-exposed body was soft and mysterious.

Yoshiko felt a mixture of shock and embarrassment, and her face betrayed her confusion.

"Don't—" she started to say. But there was no escape.

He held her wrists tightly, and within moments he had taken possession of her.

Her face tensed in a grimace, but this only made him press her down harder. The whole room seemed to be on fire. Bright flames danced around them, and she smelled the clean and pungent scent of burning citrus peels. But there was another odor as well—the intermingled scent of fish and cut grass. It was the scent of her virginity being stolen on the tatami floor. A trickle of blood stained the pale matting.

Kawashima's breathing came harshly and heavily. He thrust into her over and over, all the while continuing to lecture her solemnly on their sacred task. Righteousness was on his side!

"You are of noble blood . . . I am a man of action—" he gasped. "Nobility alone . . . is not enough to conquer the world . . . but a man of courage will also fail . . . on his own. . . . If our two bloodlines were united . . . then eugenics confirms . . . that our descendants . . . would be, without a doubt . . . heroes . . . among men. . . ."

Yoshiko was overcome by a wave of nausea.

It was early the next morning. A lilac-colored light was beginning to pale in the east. It was the same color as the panties that had been so violently torn from Yoshiko the night before. The chill of night still lingered in the air, but a new day had dawned at last.

When hope has been utterly destroyed, sometimes it is impossible to feel even sadness. Yoshiko's eyes flashed with a strange determination as she faced her mirror. She purposefully combed her hair up into a high topknot, securing it with hairpins decorated like the flowers of spring—plum blossom, cherry blossom, wisteria. She put on her favorite silk kimono. It had a design of mountains and sun on a pale pink background. She tied a peony-embroidered obi sash around her waist.

Yoshiko dressed herself carefully and elegantly. She had but one errand that morning, and that was to pay a solitary visit to a little, out-of-the-way hairdresser's far from the center of town.

When the pretty stranger arrived at the small shop, the hairdresser solicitously came out to welcome her. Handing him a camera, she instructed him to take a picture of her. There was a lush bed of chrysanthemums in front of the shop. They were in full bloom, and they made a flattering background. She gazed solemnly into the lens with an expression that was at once ceremonious and firm. There was not even the hint of a smile on her lips. She waited.

"Miss! How about a little smile?" the hairdresser coaxed.

She pretended not to hear, and the bulb flashed as he pressed the shutter button.

Inside the shop, Yoshiko faced the big mirror and loosened her topknot. Her long dark hair came tumbling down.

The hairdresser began to cut, one lock at a time. He snipped and snipped until wisps of her fallen hair covered the white cloth draped across her shoulders, until her black hair lay in thick clumps on the floor around her seat. What had once seemed to have a life of its own was now nothing more than litter, and it had all happened in the blink of an eye. This nameless hairdresser kept cutting, slowly and deliberately.

"Such a shame!" he sighed.

Yoshiko's face was like marble, cold and still.

"I would be grateful," she said with cold formality, "if you were to cut it all off. I am through with 'femininity.' "

"But, miss," he said, his face filled with regret and pity, "from now on you're going to have to wear a hairpiece."

She paid him no more heed and instead turned her attention to the woman in the mirror. She watched her hair grow shorter, and shorter, and shorter still. The hairdresser finished his task by parting her hair like a man's. The transformation was now complete. The girl she had been yesterday was dead. She had become someone else.

She got up and left, leaving the puzzled hairdresser alone. Did she really mean to adopt men's clothing, too? he wondered. What a strange girl! Whatever for? And what did she mean by that remark—"through with 'femininity'?"

6

Yamaga was full of his accustomed youthful enthusiasm and ardor as he approached their rendezvous that afternoon. But as soon as he saw her, he stopped dead in his tracks. He stared at her incredulously, without blinking. Was this Yoshiko? He was stupefied.

She wasn't wearing her usual colorful clothing this autumn evening. Instead, she was wearing a man's straight-sleeved kimono, made of blue-and-white cotton printed in a geometric design. On her feet, she wore a plain and heavy pair of wooden clogs. Her hair was incredibly short, and parted like a man's.

She had changed their meeting spot to this bamboo grove. It was her intention to break with him, cleanly and firmly. She calmly handed him a picture to remember her by. It was the one she had posed for that morning before her haircut.

Uncomprehendingly, Yamaga accepted the photo.

"But, your hair . . ." he faltered.

"The man's hand slipped, and he cut off too much."

He couldn't possibly believe that.

"What has happened?" he asked.

"There's nothing to say."

"Yoshiko," he implored, seizing her hands. "Please, tell me the truth! Tell me what's wrong!"

"I asked you to meet me here for one reason only. We can't see each other anymore!"

"Not see each other?"

He was stunned. Two days ago, everything had been just fine. And everything had been fine yesterday, as well. But she had changed overnight—into a man! And now she wanted to break with him?

"Yoshiko, no matter how much you change, my feelings for you will never change. I will always be devoted to you." He went on: "But you gave me no warning at all. Not even a hint. Even in war, one has more information than this! At least you have spies—"

"Precisely," she said flatly. "There is a war, and I am fighting in it. There is nothing I wouldn't do to further its cause, to attain the goal of an independent Manchuria."

"But you're only a woman," he said pityingly.

"Women can accomplish great things, too!" Her words were defiant, but face was expressionless. "This is what I want to do. Nobody can stop me!"

Yamaga felt his temper rising.

"All that any normal woman in the world has ever wanted

is a peaceful and happy family life. What makes you think you're so different? What kinds of adventures do you think you're going to have?"

A hundred conflicting emotions crowded her mind. Was she doing the right thing? Was she fooling herself? Could she really bear to break up with Yamaga? Did she really want to? Was her uncertainty a sign of weakness?

At last she collected herself. There was no turning back. She would simply have to get it over with.

"This is how I am," she said evenly. "It is my fate. There's nothing that can be done about it. Now, go!"

"I will wait for you, no matter how long it takes. I will make you mine."

She laughed coldly.

"I have no parents, no loved ones. I am alone; and I have no intention of ever belonging to anybody! Even if I must die, it shall be by my own hand!"

Was she so unbending? he wondered. Was there no room for compromise at all? His passion turned to fury and rose up suddenly to engulf him. His face went red with anger, and the sinews of his neck bulged tautly. Without even thinking, he drew his pistol.

"Then die!" he spat.

She took the gun from him without hesitating. Like a sleepwalker, she pointed it at her left breast and pulled the trigger. All the while, her eyes never strayed from his face.

He watched in horror as blood welled up from her wound, and a bright red stain crept across her kimono. It fanned out bit by bit like some sort of conjurer's flower.

He seized her by the wrists and pulled her to him, holding her tightly.

"I owe you nothing more!" she said emphatically.

She was animated by a weird energy. Her blood flowed rapidly from her agitated body onto his hands, and she struggled to endure the pain. It seemed to be tearing her apart, piercing right through to her very heart. She bit her lip so hard that she drew more blood. Trembling like a leaf, she tried to keep the searing pain at bay, tried to hide it away deep within her being. All of her energy was focused on one thing: She must stay conscious! She must!

At the time, she could not fully realize the significance of that gunshot. Perhaps, someday in the distant future, it might come to her in a flash of recognition. She owed him nothing! There would always be a red scar, like a tiny mole, on her left breast. Even Naniwa Kawashima, who had raped her, who had thought himself in possession of her, even he would never discover this secret.

Thirst.

She was so thirsty! It was as if she had gone a lifetime without water. Every drop of fluid in her body had been drained away, and her parched body was on fire. But it was a dim and vague kind of burning.

Yoshiko was exhausted. She dreamed she was walking down a strange road. Suddenly, it became very, very long; then, in the next instant, it started to twist and wind. On and on it stretched, without end. She tried in vain to find someone who could tell her the way; but for all eternity there was only she. And she would keep walking, and walking, forever.

She floated between consciousness and unconsciousness, caught in a struggle for her life. She fought hard, and in the end she pulled through.

Yoshiko lay on her sickbed, her face ashen. She was very weak, but she had survived.

She had no sense of how much time had passed. Was it still autumn?

Daylight would have shown a riot of fall color. The maple leaves, on the verge of turning red, shone orange and light green, like tangerines and pomelos. But inside the hospital everything was a blank and lonely white—bloodless, loveless.

Gradually, the day grew colder. The doctor came by on his rounds.

"Mr. Yamaga has come to see you many times," the doctor told Yoshiko, "but you weren't awake."

"Starting tomorrow," she said weakly, but with inner determination, "I will be receiving no visitors."

Before he could respond, she continued:

"I will be undergoing further surgery."

The doctor expressed some surprise.

"Pardon me? Miss, your operation was a success. You don't need any more surgery."

"The operation to which I am referring," she said flatly, "is a tubal ligation. I wish to be sterilized."

"What? You can't be serious!" The doctor looked at her in shock.

"Yes, I am," she said firmly. "And I shall sign for the bill myself."

"It can't be done. You won't come of age until you are twenty years old. And besides, I simply cannot—"

"If you refuse," she said, cutting him off, "then I shall kill myself. Tomorrow."

Having delivered this ultimatum to the doctor, Yoshiko turned her face away and shut her eyes. She was chasing the shadows from her spirit. She would be free.

Although she was not tall and did not appear to be physically strong, every fiber of her body was steeled with inner strength; and every ounce of that strength was directed toward one goal: making a clean break.

She could not remember when she had begun doing it, but she had long liked to chant a little poem to herself:

> I have a home I can't return to,
> I'm full of tears I cannot cry.
> The only law here is injustice,
> Who will listen to my story?

She would not die. She had to keep on living. When she reflected back over her life and thought about squaring old accounts, she realized that she did not hold anyone else accountable for her fate. Oddly, this thought terrified her. But she had paid off her debts. She was free to begin again.

7

Yoshiko Kawashima and Ganjurjab were wed in Port Arthur, Manchuria, in November of 1927. The ceremony was held at the opulent Daiwa Hotel, in the Japanese concession. The union was a great accomplishment for the staff officers of Japan's Kwantung Army, which was now poised to invade Manchuria.

Naniwa Kawashima did not attend the ceremony. He had served his purpose, and there was no longer any place for him in the enterprise. Army Headquarters was now in charge of the entire operation. It was more efficient that way. Kawashima had unwittingly given the operation a strong push at a very critical moment, but he was no longer deemed useful. The higher-ups agreed that it was best that he retire from public life. It wasn't what he had hoped for, but he had expected it for some time.

The Kwantung Army's invasion strategy had two prongs: military and civil. On the military front, Colonel Daisaku Komoto masterminded a plot to assassinate Marshal Chang Tso-lin, the powerful warlord who not only controlled Manchuria but also two other adjacent northeastern provinces. Komoto's men blew up Chang's private train car as he traveled from Peking to Mukden, killing him and thus eliminating one more obstacle in the way of Japanese domination of Manchuria.

On the civil front, the Kwantung Army helped to engineer the marriage of Yoshiko and Ganjurjab, which created a powerful alliance between the Manchurian and Mongolian peoples. Without their combined support, Japan could not hope to occupy the Northeast.

The wedding was a lavish affair, attended by an impressive list of VIPs. The chief of staff of the Kwantung Army was there, along with an assortment of officers and members of the Black Dragon Society. There were foreign ambassadors, the new head of Prince Su's household, Chinese adventurers, and even old Ching loyalists. This last group still refused to wear Western clothing, and, for this special occasion, they had rummaged through their dusty trunks and pulled out the antiquated long gowns and ceremonial robes that they now wore. Although it had been over a decade since the fall of the dynasty and the founding of the Republic, some of these old royalists had somehow managed to save their braids from the shears of zealous progressives. For the wedding today, they defiantly drew these symbols of Ching loyalty out from underneath their hats for all the world to see.

There were other holdovers from the *ancien regime* there as well. Highborn ladies came teetering in on tiny bound feet, each lady supported by several attendants. With their smooth, porcelain-white skin and their finely arched brows and almond eyes, they were the epitome of nobility and cultivation. But elegance and hauteur were all that these aristocratic ladies had—in every other respect, they were quite useless. They were helpless and crippled, for a cruel and barbaric custom had deformed their feet, which had been rolled up into little balls of flesh and broken bone. This made them completely dependent, not even able to cross their own thresholds without help, and swaying unsteadily as they hobbled down the street.

Yoshiko smiled at them coldly. She pitied them. She was not one of them. She was nothing like them. She was capable, driven, and independent. And although she was a woman, she saw herself as both masculine and feminine, possessing the best qualities of both. She would be a man among women.

Yoshiko's wedding dress was a Mandarin-collared cheongsam of multicolored satin with borders of embroidered flowers around the hem and cuffs. A long, flowing veil of diaphanous silk trailed the floor behind her, rippling as she walked.

Her face was rigid beneath drifts of heavy makeup. The stiff white powder permitted her no expression—she was like a doll made of snow. Against the dead white of her face, her crimson-painted lips looked all the more ripe and brilliant. Elaborate earrings of pearls and carved jade hung ponderously from her ears, clumsily dragging across her shoulders. In short, Yoshiko looked just like any other bride sitting primly for wedding photos with her bridegroom. Ganjurjab stood stiffly beside her, decked out in a long mandarin-collared gown, brocade jacket, and little round ceremonial cap of satin.

During a break in the festivities, Ganjurjab leaned over to Yoshiko and whispered into her ear.

"I was really surprised when you agreed to my proposal," he said, brimming with happiness.

"I was surprised myself," she answered dryly.

"I'll give you anything you ask for. Just say the word." He seemed oblivious to her icy tone.

"There's really nothing I want—except my freedom."

"Your freedom?"

She felt a trace of contempt for her new husband.

"Your noble father pledged his loyalty to mine," she explained. "For my part, I have pledged my loyalty to the Ching emperor, and to him only. If I am to keep my faith, I must have the freedom to act on my own, as I see fit. Otherwise, we will never be able to achieve the sacred task we have set out to achieve."

"But—you're my wife now!" he said indignantly. Still, Ganjurjab loved her, loved her far more than she loved him, and he could not deny her anything. "Whatever your heart desires," he said.

Just then a handful of decrepit old royalists came up to congratulate the newlyweds. These men had managed to live to a ripe old age—for nothing. The worthless servants of a vanished nation, they were filled with bitter regrets, and they faced death with the knowledge that they would go to their graves without seeing their hopes realized. Yoshiko was like a ray of hope to them: Just when they had all but given up, Manchuria was blessed by this fine flower of womanhood. Her family background was impeccable, and she was beautiful, too. They saw in her the future of Manchuria, and all of their hopes were riding on her.

"Congratulations!"

"Best wishes!"

"What a perfect couple you make!"

"The spirit of the great Ching dynasty lives on in you, Princess!"

Yoshiko inclined her head proudly, acknowledging their tribute.

"Now, just as it has been throughout history, the people are looking to young heroes like you to save them!"

"We all hope that you will succeed and that the day is not far off!"

On and on they went, heaping praise and flattery on the young couple, but at last the little delegation thinned out until they had all withdrawn. Their empty words vanished with them, as though swept away by a sandstorm on the Mongolian steppes.

Yoshiko was twenty years old when she married Ganjurjab. He was twenty-four, and, as suited a Mongolian prince, he took her home to his family after the wedding. They moved to the windswept grasslands of Mongolia, leaving the bustle and sophistication of the big city far behind.

At first Yoshiko was awed by the grandeur of the vast landscape, and she delighted in galloping on horseback over the seemingly endless plains. But there was no escaping the backwardness of life in this remote region. Yoshiko was accustomed to the constant activity and variety of city life, and she soon tired of having to face the same broad expanse of yellow dust day after day. She was high-spirited and liked excitement, and this place made her unutterably miserable.

Ganjurjab's clan was very large. Aside from her mother-in-law, Yoshiko had to contend with aunts, sisters-in-law, uncles, brothers-in-law, nephews, and other assorted relatives. To make matters worse, she and Ganjurjab were not getting along very well. They argued continually, but he always backed down and let her have her way.

What a weakling! He was a man. He was supposed to be strong and firm, but instead he always swallowed his anger and made all kinds of concessions, just to keep the peace. He loved her deeply; but the more he loved her, the more he invited her contempt.

But why did she always pick fights with him in the first place? It was all because she wasn't cut out to be an ordinary married woman. With no one to confide in, she bottled up her frustrations and became increasingly alienated from the rest of the family, who came to see her as a kind of freak.

What about her dreams of an independent Manchuria and Mongolia? What about bringing back the Ching dynasty, in all its power and glory? What did this marriage have to do with any of that?

Suddenly, she saw her mistake. She had married the wrong man. What was more, she wasn't meant for this kind of life. Why, the very idea of marriage was ridiculous to her. There were plenty of men in the world who could give her what she needed.

Ganjurjab tried to please her by moving back to Dairen, a large city on the coast of Manchuria. But Yoshiko still wasn't happy—life with Ganjurjab had become unbearable. She went on numerous car trips with an endless string of Japanese boyfriends. She danced the nights away with lounge lizards in Western suits and came traipsing home in the early hours, under the watchful eyes of neighborhood gossips. One day she came across a tabloid at the newsstand. It had a flowery masthead, and the headline read THE ROMANTIC CAREER OF MISS YOSHIKO. She had to laugh—it was all so amusing!

Yoshiko and Ganjurjab were husband and wife in name only. They appeared together in public, attending banquets and other social functions, but their hearts were separated by a bottomless chasm.

One night, Ganjurjab came home to an empty house. He had grown used to it, but that night was different, for Yoshiko was no longer in China. She was on her way to Japan.

There, on the floor of their apartment on Sheng-te Road, he found it: her discarded wedding ring, right where she had thrown it.

After three years of married life and a lot of extramarital experience, Yoshiko had matured into a very attractive young woman. For the second time in her life, she made the solitary journey east across the Sea of Japan. But this time it was different. This time it was her idea.

She wanted to see Naniwa Kawashima.

8

When Yoshiko appeared at his door, Kawashima was more than a little surprised; but he quickly hid his astonishment and behaved as though her presence were nothing unusual.

He had sold off his house in Akabane, where ambitious men had met and plotted, and he was now living in seclusion in a quiet, out-of-the-way town. Perhaps he had been born at the wrong time, for his grand schemes had all run into dead ends. Now, for all intents and purposes, he was retired.

"It's been three years since I last heard from you. I thought you were still out on the Mongolian steppes," he said, toying with her and absently stroking the kitten on his lap.

"I won't be going back to Mongolia ever again," she said.

"Are the two of you . . . divorced?"

This was a troubling prospect, indeed. Although Kawashima had withdrawn from politics, he still had a personal interest in the situation. This new development threatened to blight the project they had labored over for years, before it could even bear fruit.

"No, no. I didn't get a divorce. I just walked out!"

Kawashima seemed utterly spent and dispirited at first; but then, out of nowhere, he felt a powerful surge of anger.

"You are too impulsive! Too undisciplined! How can you possibly expect to accomplish anything meaningful for the Black Dragon Society when you can't even control yourself! Ever since the Kwantung Army assassinated Chang Tso-lin the year before last, we have been just a step away from creating an independent nation in Manchuria—a nation for you. But now, with our goal in sight, you come running back here on your own, throwing all of our efforts away!"

Yoshiko laughed coldly. She wasn't anybody's puppet! He still thought he could control her, and it made her angry—angry at him for trying to order her around now, and angry for all of the times he'd pushed her around in the past.

"I never do anything halfway," she retorted firmly. "Nor am I one to give up in the face of a little bit of difficulty. I have come back to settle accounts with you. Ganjurjab has no talent, no potential. Thanks to you, I wasted three years of my life on him—three of the best years of my life. But I don't wish to discuss that humiliating business any further. What's done is done. I've realized that if I want to accomplish anything in this life, there is only one person I can depend on: myself!"

"So you think you can be independent, do you? What sorts

of resources do you have to draw on? What will you live on?"

"My money!"

"Your money?"

Yoshiko appraised him coldly, this man who had profited so handsomely from his long association with her father. He was a greedy parasite, and had been all his life. Why had she been so unfortunate—why had she fallen into the hands of this man? If only there had been someone else to take care of her, right from the start. It all might have been different.

"As I recall," she said, "one of the properties in my father's bequest was the Lu Tien Market in Dairen. You were to collect the rents, as well as a commission. I'm aware that these make up a considerable sum."

"Mm—so they do." He drowsily closed one eye, mocking her faintly. So that was all she was after! He skillfully dissembled, for he had been practicing the art of deception for so long that there was no trace of treachery on his face.

"As you well know," he said, gazing blandly at his kitten, "revenues from that property were earmarked for the financing of the movement. I'm afraid they've already been spent for the most part. And in any case, if you want to get money from someone, don't you think a slightly better attitude on your part would be appropriate?"

Yoshiko clenched her fists tightly, and the veins on her temples bulged with anger. Her eyes were ablaze, and she struggled to remain calm.

"It's simply a matter of wisdom, of maturity," he said, smoothly shifting his gaze toward her.

But she swept out of the room before he finished speaking, and she never looked back.

Kawashima was a dead end. It was obvious that she wasn't

going to get anything out of him. But there was still another man who just might be able to help her.

That evening, Yoshiko paid a visit to the Peony Inn. She was not the type of guest this wine-and-geisha house usually entertained. She came to find someone.

A maid led Yoshiko to one of the guest rooms, pausing briefly outside the sliding shoji door before knocking lightly. The sound of voices came from within, but no one responded to the knock. Before the girl could turn to consult with her, Yoshiko roughly slid open the door, tearing its delicate rice-paper covering.

What she saw disgusted her. It was a scene of complete depravity. The first thing she noticed was Yamaga's drunken body sprawled across the floor. His handsome, classic features seemed fuzzy and distorted, and in the gentle lamplight she barely recognized him.

His head lay pillowed on the thigh of a geisha, whose flimsy kimono was tangled around her limbs and body and was coming apart at the seams. Geisha style, her entire face and neck were covered in white greasepaint, all the way down to where the collar of her kimono should have been. But her robe had slipped, exposing a patch of the naked skin of her back. There was a mottled triangle of greasepaint at the nape of her neck, where she had half sweated it off.

She was feeding him rice wine, mouth to mouth, like a mother bird feeding her chick. The wine was scalding hot, and so she took one sip at a time, cooling the liquid in her own mouth before passing it slowly and sensuously from her lips to his. He had slipped a hand inside her kimono and was fondling her breasts as he drank. They giggled foolishly, and Yoshiko was filled with revulsion.

A flicker of motion caught Yoshiko's eye. She looked toward the other side of the room and saw a pair of half-naked geisha girls dancing seductively and making arcs in the air with gold-painted fans.

The room reeked of lust and debauchery, a wild, animal scent.

Yamaga languidly turned his eyes in the direction of the intruder and realized with a start that it was Yoshiko! Yet in his stupor he was not sure that she wasn't a figment of his drunken imagination. Propping himself up on one elbow, he called out to her.

"Yoshiko?"

Angry and disgusted, she turned away and stormed out. After their breakup, Yoshiko had heard that Yamaga sank deeply into a life of drink and women, spending his nights and days in geisha houses. He had fallen heavily into debt, even embezzling public money to pay for his vices, or so it was said. Still, rumors were only rumors, after all, and Yoshiko clung to that one last shred of hope: that the gossip was not true. But when she saw him with her own eyes, saw how far he had fallen, her hopes were shattered in an instant.

She left Yamaga's room in a hurry, but troubling thoughts slowed her steps as she made her way out of the inn. She felt the weight of her disillusionment. Yamaga, once so strong, was now too drunk even to stand up. He had become weak, too weak to pursue her and find out if she was real or only a phantom.

Yoshiko lingered in front of the wineshop for a while, biting her lip in thought, until at last she reached a decision. She would leave this place, for good.

Neither of the men she had gone to for help were of any use to her. One had no power, and the other had no money. The

Chinese had a saying: "Great men don't fall out of power over-night, and ordinary men don't go broke overnight." It was the lesson of thousands of years of failures, and it could not have been more true.

She took a hard look at her present situation and sifted through it. In the end, all that she had left was herself. There was no one else, nothing else, she could depend on.

She wasn't about to let herself fall apart now! Never! She had an idea: There was another way out.

One afternoon, not long after her disappointing encounter with Yamaga, Yoshiko sat in a tea shop, opposite a Japanese gentleman. She had sought him out, and now here she was. She had put on a yellow cheongsam and combed her short hair carefully for the occasion. She looked quite refined and well bred as she daintily lifted her teacup and took a sip of tea.

The man sitting across from her was a famous Japanese novelist named Shofu Muramatsu.

Yoshiko did not bother to get an appointment, but went to see him directly instead, catching up with him in the tea shop she knew he frequented. Once she was settled in her seat across from him, she skipped over the small talk and spoke straight to the point.

"I have a business proposition for you," she stated levelly. "I would like to sell you a story, a very interesting and exciting story, which you may use as a plot for one of your novels. All I ask in return is the cost of a boat ticket."

Muramatsu was taken aback by her boldness; but he was rather intrigued as well.

"The protagonist of this tale," she continued, "is the four-teenth princess of the house of the Manchu prince Su, a member of the Ching royal family, which, until recently, ruled all of China. Her name is Yoshiko Kawashima."

"I see," he said, nodding in recognition, for her name had been known to him for some time.

She went on to outline the main points of the tale.

"She's a very romantic figure, a legend in her own time. Her first love is a dashing young officer from Matsumoto, but the affair ends tragically. Soon after, she marries a Mongolian prince, but the marriage doesn't last long. Wouldn't you be willing to pay good money for the details of a story like this? Wouldn't it be worth a fair amount to you—say, about two thousand yen?"

Muramatsu's response was scarcely audible, as though he were talking the matter over with himself.

"Yes," he said in a contemplative tone, "It's promising . . . 'Venus in a Suit' . . . Not a bad subject at all . . . Still—"

"What's the catch?" she asked.

"Well, quite frankly," the novelist replied, "I'm a little bit concerned about accuracy. You're offering to tell me the intimate details of someone else's life. How can I be sure—"

"You don't have to worry about that!" Yoshiko cut in. "The story in question is the story of my life."

"You're Yoshiko?" he exclaimed. "Your reputation precedes you, young lady. Why, you're the talk of the town!"

She was in no mood for polite flattery.

"All I need is two thousand yen," she told him bluntly. She could not have made it any clearer. She knew what she wanted and did not like to waste time.

In this way, Yoshiko managed to make a fresh start. *Venus in a Suit* created quite a sensation. First it was serialized in a magazine, and later it was published as a book, which quickly became a best-seller. Novelists are, as a rule, experts at the art of embellishment, and Muramatsu was certainly no exception. He skillfully fleshed out Yoshiko's brief and romantic life with numerous colorful descriptions, so that her exploits became even more lurid and fascinating.

The novel was a huge success, but Yoshiko was not there to bask in the limelight, for she had already left Japan. She had her stake, and she wagered it on the passage to China.

After Yoshiko left Japan, Yamaga received a packet, special delivery. When he opened the envelope, a stack of bills came tumbling out—one thousand yen in all. Enclosed in the packet there was also a letter:

Mr. Yamaga:

By the time you receive this letter, I will already be in China. I am going to Shanghai to make a fresh start and seek my fortune. It's time I got serious about something, and I plan to devote myself wholeheartedly to advancing the Manchu cause.

I am giving you half of all the money I have. Consider my debt to you repaid. I hope that you will pull yourself together. Remember that you are a man—and any man worth the name has no business wasting his time with geishas while destiny passes him by. We must all strive to fulfill our destinies; in the end only heaven can decide who will succeed and who will fail!"

Yoshiko had left Japan without saying good-bye to Naniwa Kawashima. She had no intention of ever seeing him again. Still, she had other ways of letting him know where she stood.

Kawashima awakened one morning to find his little kitten lying stiff and cold on the front porch. She was such a pretty little thing. Her entire body was pure white, except for an inky smudge on her forehead. So soft, so gentle, so innocent—she was like a woman. Kawashima had always preferred female animals—they made the best pets.

The kitten had been strangled with a piece of rope. It had taken only a gentle tug to break her delicate neck.

9

The beautiful city of Shanghai was coming into Yoshiko's view, and a faintly mischievous smile played about her lips as the ship entered the harbor. It would be a long time before Kawashima recovered from the shock she gave him, and she didn't even have to draw blood. All her anger toward him had been released in one bloodless act of vengeance.

The boat approached the dock. Morning mists still hovered over the Whampoa River like a pall of smoke. The Whampoa River! The Bund! These names conjured up visions of legendary Shanghai, the playground of adventurers and tycoons.

Fleets of barges plied the waters of the Whampoa, busily shuttling back and forth as they engaged in the very serious game of making money. The winners of this game were those who bought low, sold high, and knew how to use the other players.

The steamer sounded its loud horn, and Yoshiko turned her face into the morning breeze, inhaling deeply. She was her own mistress, and the time had come for her to make her first move. Just then she spotted the Shanghai clock tower. It was a lucky omen, she thought to herself.

The docks were abustle in the gray light of early morning, as people swarmed on and off of the many freighters and steamers moored there. The port of Shanghai was a hub of international activity, and people from all over the world passed through: Chinese, Japanese, Americans, British, Russians, and French. The city drew people from all walks of life as well, everyone from merchants and financiers to drug smugglers, missionaries, and students. Shanghai was open to anyone who was willing to try his luck, for there were plenty of spoils to go around. It was 1931, and while Shanghai seemed to thrive, China was on the brink of disaster.

There were missionaries on the quay handing out leaflets with pictures of a Caucasian Jesus nailed to his cross. The bold-printed caption read LOVE GOD!

Passersby took these leaflets, barely giving them a glance before one of the students standing close by thrust another leaflet into their hands. Unlike the missionaries' leaflets, those of the students had no pictures and were simple mimeographed sheets crowded with cramped handwritten characters. But even if the package was messy and jumbled, the message was clear enough: LOVE CHINA!

Of course, many people only loved money. After all, God always seemed to punish the common people; and nations often abandoned their own people. But money was different: Money, and money alone, was incapable of ingratitude. If you had money, you could hail a pedicab to cart you around, or hire a coolie to haul your heavy bags. In short, money produced results.

Yoshiko was from the North, and this southern port city was, in many ways, like a foreign country full of strange sights and sounds. But she was well accustomed to traveling alone, and she did not feel disconcerted in the least. The only thing she had to worry about was finding lodgings for the night. Despite several days and nights on board ship, she felt full of energy, and easily lifted her small suitcase, scanning the scene around her.

A pair of pedicabs came rolling up, manned by two young men who had been waiting nearby to meet the arriving steamer. The men began to load huge trunks, each emblazoned with a big, bright character, the name "Tuan." Yoshiko watched the pair with curiosity, and one of them flashed her a smile.

The trunks belonged to a Peking opera company, and they were packed with costumes and props. "Tuan" must have been one of the star performers, and this pair of strong young men were probably apprentice actors. It was the younger of the two who caught Yoshiko's eye. She could tell he was the younger because of the way the other man was ordering him around.

The junior actor moved agilely, with the perfect grace and economy of motion of someone who had spent years practicing the acrobatics of Chinese opera. It was a joy to watch him perform even a menial task, and what a cute face! One look at his boyishly mischievous smile, and Yoshiko just had to like him. Who could ever be angry with someone who smiled like that?

The senior apprentice was speaking to him, telling him to get back to work. He nodded his assent and hoisted another trunk.

Yoshiko kept watching him. He was handsome and funny, both at the same time. He was such a ham that he did not mind putting on a show for an audience of only one; when he saw that Yoshiko was still watching, he took to clowning around in earnest. Hefting a trunk onto his shoulders, he affected the exaggeratedly rolling, high-stomping walk of a Peking opera general. He struck a martial pose, then strutted over to the cart, an actor playing to his devoted fans.

"Hey! Watch out!" the senior apprentice yelled. "Those trunks are full of valuable props! Be careful!"

"Yes-s-sir!" the young fellow replied, still hamming it up.

How full of vitality he was, Yoshiko thought to herself. Such thick, masculine eyebrows and such a twinkle in his eyes! She hadn't seen a man like this in ages, one so pure and full of energy. He was like a young eagle emerging from his nest and stretching his wings before he learned to fly. He still had that air of vulnerability and could not have been much over twenty.

But Yoshiko was shaken out of her reverie by a tramp who appeared out of nowhere and accosted her. Planting himself directly in front of her, he glared menacingly. Before Yoshiko had time to react, he roughly tore her purse from her hands and sped away, leaving her too startled to scream.

The thief ran like the wind—smack, right into the young actor, who went flying. The trunk he was carrying came crashing down and burst open, scattering costumes everywhere. Not one to stand by while a poor, defenseless woman was taken advantage of by a vile rogue, the actor picked himself up and sprang onto his pedicab in hot pursuit of the villain.

Since a pedicab is far quicker than a man on foot, the hero caught up with the thief in no time, and a terrible fight ensued. A couple of rickshaws were knocked over in the struggle, as the thief tried in vain to escape, but he was no match for the strapping young man. After a few rounds, the actor wrested the purse from the thief.

When the young fellow came back to return Yoshiko's stolen property, he was rather concerned that this delicate and refined young lady might have taken a fright.

"There's nothing to be afraid of now, miss. It's all over," he said soothingly. "Please, take a look and make sure that everything is there."

Yoshiko opened the purse and pulled out a thick bundle of Japanese yen. It was all that she owned.

"Oh! You're Japanese?" His heart sank. He tried the only Japanese word he knew.

"*Sayonara! Sayonara!*"

"Thank you," Yoshiko said in Chinese, and smiled at him as she snapped shut her purse.

He was overjoyed to hear her speaking Chinese, and he fairly beamed with delight.

"Phew! What a relief. So you're Chinese after all!" he sighed.

He scratched his head, racking his brains for ways to keep the conversation going. What could he talk about?

"Um, miss," he ventured, "what brings you to Shanghai? Trying to make it in the big city? . . . Hey, me, too! Why, I—"

"Ah-fu!" the senior apprentice yelled out to him. The elder fellow thought his charge was getting more than a bit too carried away with with his role of "knight in shining armor." The lady had her belongings back, and that should have been the end of it. But there he stood, dithering around and taking his own sweet time in getting back to work.

"Ah-fu! You caught the thief, so why don't you get back to business! I think the fair maiden has conquered the knight this time!"

The young actor was visibly embarrassed. But it wasn't the

77

teasing about knights and maidens that bothered him—no, it was that ridiculous nickname, Ah-fu. It made him cringe.

"I suppose you heard what he called me," he said awkwardly.

"I heard."

"Ugh! That name! 'Ah-fu' makes me sound like some sort of country bumpkin! But I have a . . . a stage name!"

Yoshiko smiled at his sweet sincerity. He didn't have the faintest idea who she was. He treated her the way he would have treated anyone else and had no preconceived notions about her. They were complete strangers, and they could not use each other. A relationship this simple and straightforward was a strange and new experience for her.

"Thank-you, Ah-fu," she said, adding with emphasis: "Good-bye!"

Cool and polite, she turned and walked away.

The actor felt torn. On one hand he felt angry and cursed the elder apprentice under his breath, muttering, "You dog breath! See if I don't beat you up later!" But he also felt deeply disappointed as he helplessly watched her move away.

"Miss!" he called out after her.

Yoshiko paused, turning to look at him.

"Remember," he said, as if in benediction, " 'Wait for the parting clouds, and you will see the bright moon!' "

"Sure. That's only common sense, isn't it?"

This time she did not turn around again, and he watched her back recede until it disappeared into the crowd.

"Hey! Hey! Sleepless nights ahead thinking about someone special, eh?"

Ah-fu paid no attention, for he was aware only of his own sadness. She was gone, without a trace. Had she come to Shanghai to search for her relatives? Or had she come in search of work? He would never know. Making it big in Shanghai—that was easier said than done!

Shanghai was a city like no other. Although it was a Chinese city, it had little in common with China's other big cities. Shanghai was the most modern Chinese city, and it was also the most dangerous, wicked, and debauched. It had everything: opulent hotels and restaurants, nightclubs, dance halls, theaters, and department stores. There were jai-alai arenas, racetracks, strip joints, opium dens, and brothels. There were neighborhoods full of splendid mansions set in lush gardens. But behind this glittering facade were stinking alleys lined with hovels and the corpses of the starved. Here dwelt men and women who would sell anything just to stay alive: their bodies, their self-respect, their youth, their strength, even their souls. They had no choice if they wanted to survive.

Shanghai's foreign concessions were known the world over as a paradise—but only for foreigners, not Chinese. Foreign nationals lived there, beyond the reach of Chinese laws, on land "ceded" by a humiliated China after the Opium Wars. There was a park in the British concession along the Whampoa River with a sign posted at its front gate that read NO CHINESE OR DOGS ALLOWED.

In spite of, or perhaps because of, all this, Shanghai was a magnet for China's revolutionary leaders. But the city attracted movers and shakers from other nations as well, especially politicians and military men.

Anything was possible in this city of vice and enchantment, and it was filled with opportunities for an ambitious young temptress like Yoshiko. As it turned out, she did not have to wait long for an opportunity to exploit, and the Mitsui Products

Corporation's annual gala ball was just the opening she was waiting for.

Waltz music filled the grand hall with its overripe cadences, adding to the extravagant atmosphere. The guest list of this ball was a Who's Who of Japanese society.

Mitsui Products was a subsidiary of the Mitsui Investment Group, which the parent corporation had set up to exploit economic opportunities in China. Ever since its establishment in China some two decades before, Mitsui Products had hosted a yearly gala. High-ranking military and civil officials always topped the guest list, and this year's guests were even more illustrious than usual. When these men thought about exploiting China, they did not just think about the balance of trade. Their ambitions toward China went much further.

Yoshiko chose this occasion for her first public appearance, and she showed up in a dazzling gown. She was the talk of the ball, and she danced beautifully, too. The waltz step was a perfect vehicle for Yoshiko's sexuality, as she gracefully whirled around the dance floor with her bright gown fluttering about her. She changed partners many times, gliding from man to man. All eyes were on her, and soon a circle of handsome admirers gathered to watch her. Multitiered chandeliers blazed above her, their hanging crystals trembling like tassels and showering her with a shimmering light.

But Yoshiko did not come just to dance, and her entire performance was targeted at one man: Shunkichi Uno. Yoshiko researched him and learned that Uno held the rank of commander in Japan's Army of conquest, the North China Expeditionary Force, and that he was currently posted to the Japanese Consulate in Shanghai. But his real work consisted of running a network of spies, and that was why she chose him.

Yoshiko caught a glimpse of Uno out of the corner of her eye as she danced. Although he was in his fifties, he looked more like a man of forty and was clearly still in his prime. Tall and somewhat forbidding, he seemed to look down on those around him from a remote height. And something in his features suggested a streak of sadism. He wore his hair clipped back very short, and with his bristly hair and his well-tailored Western suit, Uno looked modern and poised. From time to time, he would throw back his head and give a loud and lusty laugh, but that laugh had a cutting tone that invariably made his companions look as though they had been slapped in the face.

Yoshiko walked nonchalantly over to where he stood and looked at him without saying anything. Uno gazed back steadily, without expression. The two of them had not danced together yet, and they took each other's hands, each testing the other's strength. Just as Uno was about to introduce himself, Yoshiko flitted away to another dancing partner.

Later in the evening, an announcement went out over the public-address system.

"Ladies and gentlemen. The Queen of the Waltz at this year's gala ball has been chosen. And the lovely lady is Miss Yoshiko Kawashima!"

There was enthusiastic applause, but nobody went up to the podium to accept the award. Yoshiko Kawashima was nowhere to be found.

Shunkichi Uno distractedly swirled the fine amber brandy in his glass. Raising his eyes, he searched every corner of the room, but there was no trace of her. He spent the remainder of the evening in a state of restless agitation, looking up periodically to scan the hall. He never found her. He felt as if he had lost something but carried on as before, throwing his head back in laughter and pretending to take pleasure in the company of his colleagues.

The day after the waltz, Uno was at his office, with his head buried in the paperwork that had piled up on his desk, when there was a knock on the door. He raised his head.

It was Yoshiko.

She showed up completely unannounced. People who wished to see Uno ordinarily went through the proper channels, and he was accustomed to being notified of visitors in advance. But this young woman had come directly to headquarters without any introduction, and had walked straight into the room and sat down opposite him at his desk.

Overnight, she had undergone a complete transformation. On the previous evening, she had worn an elegant French ball gown. Today, she was dressed in a Chinese cheongsam. Modestly attired in this perfectly fitted garment, she had the restrained coquettishness of a Chinese girl.

Uno had done some research of his own since last night.

"So, Miss Yoshiko, how did you manage to disappear into thin air?"

"I show up when it's important, don't I?" She laughed.

He laughed, too.

"This is quite unexpected—but most flattering!" He winked.

"Perhaps I've come at an inconvenient time?"

Shunkichi Uno stood up and walked over to his liquor cabinet.

"It's not that," he said, picking up a bottle of three-star brandy. "You simply should have let me know that you were coming. Tea? Or brandy?"

Without waiting for an answer, he poured two glasses of brandy.

She raised her chin almost imperceptibly and said provocatively:

"I would like you to be my sponsor, Mr. Uno!"

She was neither groveling nor arrogant, and her eyes were filled with mirth, but there was nothing spontaneous about her expression. She spent many hours in front of her mirror practicing every smile possible. Once each smile was tried and perfected, she filed it away in her memory until such time as she needed it. Today, she chose this particular smile.

"Why do you want my protection? Is somebody giving you trouble?" he asked.

"No, it's not that. It's just that I'm tired of all these silly men coming around to waste my time. As you're well aware, Mr. Uno, time is a precious commodity. A woman's time is the most valuable of all."

"Women have always had to contend with unwanted male attentions, and they always will. I'm sure that that's especially true for you, Miss Yoshiko." He was no longer smiling. "But the truth of the matter is that you have been capitalizing on this situation and taking advantage of your social standing to do so, my dear 'Princess.' "

"Please, call me Yoshiko. I shall call you 'Father,' " she said with false sincerity. She was using her social "capital" at this very moment, just as she used it all the time, implicitly and confidently. "Father" was a respectful form of address, but there was nothing respectful about the way she said it.

"May I refuse?" he asked. "After all, even the slightest impropriety between father and daughter would be incest!"

"Incest!" she exclaimed. "How can you even speak of such a thing?"

Uno gave a hearty laugh.

"We can still dance together," she said, giving him a scathing look, but Uno kept laughing.

He was dangerous and crafty, and she knew it. But he was also very powerful. That was what had attracted her to him, for she hoped to use his power to achieve her own ends.

10

A chauffeur-driven car sped through the outskirts of Shanghai. Yoshiko and Uno were riding in the back.

They followed the road into some woods, and suddenly they were in another world, another time. The noise and tumult of the city were like a distant dream. Lush trees arched overhead, bright with green leaves. Flowers blazed in their brief season.

Deep in the woods the car came to an abrupt halt, and Yoshiko felt a touch of apprehension. Neither she nor Uno spoke at first.

It was Uno who broke the silence.

"Where are you living?"

"I've just started to look for a place," she answered him, but she was thinking how strange it was that they had stopped here, in this isolated patch of forest.

As Uno's breathing grew more rapid, Yoshiko realized what was going on. So that was it. After all, what man would be content to share just a glass of brandy with her? The driver pretended not to notice the drama unfolding in the backseat. He sat like a statue, staring straight ahead and minding his own business, a loyal servant.

Yoshiko started to hum softly. It was a haunting tune, full of yearning, but it also had a vaguely lilting quality, like a waltz.

"Shall we dance, Father?" she asked. She didn't look directly at him, but she flashed him an oddly intriguing look as she turned and slid out of the car. She extended her leg, exposing a garter, and stood up slowly before making her way toward the trees, her hips swaying to some inner music.

She turned to face her opponent, but he was right behind her. Yoshiko placed her hands lightly on his shoulders and danced a few steps, concentrating on her dancing.

"Let's just dance," she said firmly.

Yoshiko felt a jerk as Uno pulled out a pistol. She jumped back and eyed him warily, unable to read his thoughts. His eyes burned through her malevolently.

She stepped back a few paces but was blocked by the trunk of a large tree. Uno pressed close and poked his gun into her abdomen as he tore off her skirt and ripped away the waistband with his free hand.

Yoshiko lost all sense of time and place. There was nothing but the sun-dappled trees trembling above. The sun shone down through gaps in the dancing leaves, painting their two bodies with a pattern of light and shadow. She felt exposed, as though all of heaven and earth were watching them.

Uno sprang his trap on her when she least expected it. Caught off guard, she struggled to break away, but the pistol butt only dug harder into her flesh, and she gradually surrendered to her feelings of helplessness and let her eyelids close. She felt like a piece of meat pinned against the rough bark of the tree, and the pain and humiliation showed on her face.

Her submissive and miserable expression made Uno feel even more powerful and potent. He was the king of beasts, the conquering soldier, the great man. He violated Yoshiko without warning or preliminary, like an animal. All men were the same, she thought. She strained to twist away from the pain and bit down hard on her lower lip, refusing to let out even the hint of a moan.

Uno made no attempt at concealment; they were completely exposed in the open air. The sun shone down on their two bodies, locked together, half standing.

She lost track of the cold metal nose of the pistol, but she knew it was still there. She also knew that one false move would be the end of her, and her fear and the threat of the unseen gun incapacitated her.

He crushed her body against his own, reveling in his power, a common rapist. She realized that it was a lust to dominate that drove him. If she wanted to stay alive, she would have to satisfy that desire in him. He must think he had completely subjugated her, and so she allowed her expression to grow ever more abject, ever more ashamed. She would let him think he had conquered her. She gave him what he wanted and lured him in, although it hurt her.

Through the pain she felt a secret pleasure, the pleasure of controlling him without his knowledge. A grassy odor in the air brought back the memory of that fateful evening in Kawashima's study. But this time it was different—this time it was she who was in control.

And then he came, like a gunshot fired by a sniper, and she found herself crying out with him, a tangled and excited cry.

Guns fired and shouts rang out over the battlefield. Japan was invading Manchuria.

At 10:20 on the evening of September 18, 1931, the Kwantung Army carried out an act of provocation that became known as the September Eighteenth Incident.

Japanese engineers dynamited a section of railroad track north of the Manchurian city of Shenyang, destroying the track and damaging a train. Japanese officials blamed the incident on the Chinese Army, and, on this pretext, the Kwantung Army began firing on the Chinese garrison at Peitaying. The Japanese commander then gave the order to launch the assault, and the Japanese Army brazenly drove deep into Manchuria. The invasion had officially begun, but the Chinese troops stationed in Manchuria were under orders from Chiang Kai-shek not to resist, and they fled in disarray back to China proper.

After the September Eighteenth Incident, the Japanese invasion was launched on a big scale. In the following year, the entire region of Manchuria fell to Japan's Kwantung Army. With Manchuria securely in its control, the army could do with it whatever it pleased. It was the springboard to total domination of Asia.

Although the Japanese were firmly in possession of the region, they still lacked one thing—a pretty package to wrap it all up in, some way to dress up their naked aggression. So they sent Colonel Kenji Tohibara to Tientsin to meet with the deposed Ching emperor, Pu-yi.

The last emperor was living as an ordinary citizen at a villa he had named the Garden of Tranquillity, where he was still attended by a retinue of old Ching loyalists who saw to his every need and refused to leave his side. His hopes of restoration rose and fell with the political tides; although the Ching dynasty was long since dead and buried, Pu-yi's Japanese associates continually assured him that restoration was not a lost cause. They insisted that he look after his health, so that he would be prepared when the time came for him to rule once more.

Although Pu-yi's advisers constantly gave him optimistic reports, China was in total political chaos, with faction pitted against faction in a confusing array of shifting alliances. Today's friend became tomorrow's enemy. No one could be trusted. With the nation growing more fragmented and unstable day by day, the very idea of "unifying" China seemed an absurd fantasy, but Pu-yi lived in a fool's paradise.

He was a self-indulgent and profligate man, every month spending vast sums of money on presents for himself and the empress. He bought her everything from pianos, clocks, and radios to imported clothing, leather shoes, eyeglasses, diamonds, and even cars. Pu-yi also had a weakness for fortune-tellers and mediums, and he especially liked to consult the I-ching. They always told him what he wanted to hear, promising vast power and riches.

Now, at last, his wishes were coming true! The Japanese had sent an emissary—they were going to help him.

Colonel Tohibara was a fiftyish man with a goatee who gave a polite and pleasant impression in spite of his rather droopy eyelids. He presented himself to Pu-yi. After a few polite formalities, he stated his business.

"Your Manchurian homeland was in dire straits. That warlord Chang Hsueh-liang misgoverned it terribly, leaving the region impoverished and politically unstable. This situation was a threat to the interests and property of my Japanese countrymen there, so my nation was left with no alternative but to send in troops to protect our citizens and property. Of course, in the long term, the Kwantung Army is sincerely committed to helping the people of Manchuria establish their independence. But the new Manchurian nation will need a leader."

He paused briefly before adding, "His Imperial Highness, the emperor of Japan, has lent us his full support. He has absolute faith in our Kwantung Army!"

"If you will return me to my rightful station as emperor, I will agree to go to Manchuria. Otherwise, I shall refuse," Pu-yi insisted.

"Why, of course we plan to restore the monarchy," Tohibara replied. He smiled faintly, but his voice remained even. "That goes without saying."

Tohibara's calm attitude hid the fact that getting Pu-yi to Manchuria was a matter of extreme urgency to the Japanese. It was to be done as soon as possible, and Tohibara was simply pandering to Pu-yi's ambition in order to get his cooperation. Once Pu-yi reached Manchuria, he would be nothing but a puppet emperor. But Pu-yi was too blinded by ambition even to suspect their true intentions.

On a dark November night, a small motorboat neared the shore at the Manchurian port city of Yingkou. The vessel, the *Hijiyama Maru,* belonged to the Transport Division of Japanese Military Headquarters. Its mission had been to transport Pu-yi from Tientsin under the strictest security, and the crew had never let him out of their sight.

All was dark and quiet on shore, and nothing could be seen

in the gloom except a few figures waiting nervously in the shadows. The only other sign of life was the occasional half-hearted barking of a dog somewhere in the distance.

Yoshiko and Shunkichi Uno stood together, watching with bated breath the little black dot that hugged the shore. They were flanked by aides-de-camp, a few military policemen, and Uno's special aide, whose tightly pursed lips only detracted slightly from his rather handsome features. He had a resourceful and determined air, indeed. This Chinese orphan raised by Japanese troops was known for his quick wits and cool head. He had come far and held many important duties in Uno's organization. His family name was Lin, and everybody called him by the nickname Hsiao Lin, or Young Lin.

Young Lin's eyes did not waver from the small motorboat as it docked.

Yoshiko gave him a quick appraisal. A young Chinese man working with China's sworn enemies, the Japanese? That was highly unusual, abnormal even, she thought to herself.

The boat's passengers started to disembark. Cheng Hsiao-hsu, a politician, and his son led the way, followed by several of Pu-yi's loyal retainers, a few Japanese officers, and a dozen other soldiers. Pu-yi, disguised in a Japanese Army coat and cap, was the last to appear. He looked haggard, as though there'd been trouble along the way; but now he thought he had found a safe harbor at last.

The welcoming party rushed forward to greet Pu-yi and pay their respects as he stepped ashore.

"Your Imperial Highness has undoubtedly had a difficult journey," Uno said as he saluted. "Tonight, we will travel by car to the hot springs at Tang Peak. After a few days' rest, we will proceed to Port Arthur."

Pu-yi surveyed the small group assembled before him. Was

this the full extent of his welcoming party? he wondered with some disappointment. He still had on dark glasses, and when he pulled a long face, his entire body seemed cloaked in gloom. But then a ray of light burst upon the company, and right before his eyes there stood a beautiful young woman. She came forward and presented herself.

"Best wishes to Your Imperial Highness," she said, all but prostrating herself before him. "Hsien-tzu, the fourteenth daughter of Prince Su, at Your Majesty's service."

Pu-yi brightened visibly at the sight of his countrywoman. She was like him—a Manchu, and a member of the Ching imperial clan.

"Hm. I seem to remember you. You are my cousin, are you not?" he said.

Yoshiko felt a flush of pride at being singled out by the emperor. In a crowd of Japanese men, it was she, Yoshiko, who was the emperor's favorite. But she carefully hid her pleasure, responding to Pu-yi in a voice that betrayed nothing.

"Your Highness flatters me. Although I am still known by some as Hsien-tzu, I have a *nom de guerre*—Yoshiko Kawashima," she said, ambition shining in her eyes.

Members of the imperial household crowded in behind the emperor. Their future and the future of the Ching dynasty depended on Yoshiko and a handful of foreign strangers.

"Your Highness can rest assured," Uno said warmly. "We are committed to the great task of founding an independent Manchuria."

As Pu-yi was escorted to a waiting carriage, he turned to Yoshiko.

"I had expected a bigger crowd," he confided morosely, "all waving flags and cheering. . . ."

"Your Highness, when the time comes, there most assuredly will be," Yoshiko replied in a firm and masculine tone.

As Pu-yi mounted the carriage, she turned to Uno's special aide.

"Young Lin! Protect His Majesty well!" she commanded.

"Yes, ma'am!" he answered heartily.

Pu-yi needed protection—only a day before his departure from Tientsin, there was an attempt on his life. A fruit basket had arrived at his residence, and closer inspection had revealed that there were explosives hidden inside. This narrow escape left Pu-yi feeling especially anxious to leave Tientsin, but perhaps the timing was too perfect. After all, nobody knew for sure who sent the explosive package. It might well have been a Japanese ruse to frighten Pu-yi and speed him on his way to Manchuria.

The group watched Pu-yi's carriage until it was out of sight, and then Uno walked over to Yoshiko. They stood face-to-face, eyeing each other momentarily, a pair of wary conspirators. Both were troubled by the same question: Where was the empress Wan-jung? Why hadn't she come to Manchuria with her husband?

Yoshiko was back in her old home, Port Arthur. The pain of being sent away at the age of seven had all but faded from her memory, but she could still remember her childhood in this city. She and her thirty-odd brothers and sisters did everything together—they played in the garden, catching sparrows, gathering wild dates, or waiting eagerly for the apricot blossoms of spring. They studied together, too, learning Chinese, Japanese, and calligraphy. But, suddenly, everything had changed, and she was thrown into a new life. Her childhood ended the day she boarded the ship to Japan.

At twenty she came back here and became a married woman. What pomp and fanfare accompanied that event! Of course, it did not last, and now she was a divorcée. Such are the vicissitudes of fate.

Despite all that happened here, she did not think of Port Arthur as her true home, but rather as a way station.

This time around, Yoshiko stayed at the Daiwa Hotel, that fancy Japanese establishment where she was married. Pu-yi was sequestered on the upper floor, along with a small entourage. Until his coronation, he was to remain there, for all purposes under house arrest. While he was essentially a Japanese prisoner, they treated him with the utmost respect.

It was three o'clock in the morning, and there were only two customers in the hotel's elegant and spacious bar. Guards kept watch over the vast hall.

Yoshiko and Shunkichi Uno had been up all night. He was pacing slowly, his hands clasped behind his back. She sat on a barstool, lost in thought. They were both worrying about the same problem: the last empress, Wan-jung.

"Every play needs a hero and a heroine," Uno muttered to himself.

"What do you mean, 'play'? You make the founding of Manchukuo sound like an amateur theatrical!" Yoshiko said indignantly. She was also thinking that every play has a final curtain, and that the curtain must never fall on the Ching dynasty.

Yoshiko and Uno were already at cross-purposes, although they continued to plot and scheme together and kept ulterior motives hidden.

Uno brought the topic of conversation back to the empress.

"What's your guess?" he asked her. "Why do you think the

empress didn't come to Manchuria with the emperor?"

"From what I've gathered, she didn't come because she didn't want to."

"Yes, but was that her idea or the emperor's?"

It was a fair question, for it was common knowledge that the emperor and empress had become estranged. Pu-yi was intoxicated by dreams of returning to his dragon throne, and there was no room in his heart for anything but restoration of the Ching dynasty. It was a passion that controlled his life. During his time in Tientsin, Pu-yi played host to an endless parade of guests—militarists, politicians, even foreigners. Some of them were rather unsavory characters, but he welcomed them all, provided they expressed a willingness to aid him in his cause. When he had money, he paid these "supporters" handsomely. When there was no cash on hand, he gave them artifacts from the imperial collection. He handed out everything from pearls and jewels to antiques, paintings, and calligraphy scrolls, as "tokens of appreciation."

The empress, the imperial consort, and the rest of Pu-yi's concubines faded into the background, like so much furniture. Pu-yi neglected his marital relationships to such a point that his wives felt like little more than slaves. The emperor's consort, Wen-hsiu, found the situation so unbearable that she filed for divorce. But the empress Wan-jung did not leave. A member of one of the most powerful Manchu clans, she had entered the imperial court at the age of seventeen, and it was not easy for her to leave. Furthermore, the title of empress still meant a great deal to her, and she held fast to this faded remnant of China's feudal past.

Clinging to her privilege for dear life, Wan-jung grew more narrow-minded and obsessive with each day, and became superstitious to the point of madness. A jealous woman, she could not tolerate the presence of other women. The emperor, for his part, could not tolerate her. Sinking ever deeper into depression, she took to smoking opium and soon became heavily addicted. At the same time, rumors began to circulate about her loose morals. Once the empress of a vast nation, Wan-jung was a pathetic figure.

"Well, in any case," Yoshiko was saying to Uno, "this grand scheme of ours can hardly come off without Wan-jung. The stage will be as good as empty if the heroine doesn't show up!" She laughed ruefully.

Uno seemed to consider for a moment.

"If only there were someone," he said without looking at her, "someone bold enough, bold enough to risk going to Tient-sin in secret to bring back the empress—"

"That someone is me," Yoshiko broke in. "I'm the one for the job. I know it."

"It would be a very dangerous operation. Why you?"

"Because I've been waiting for a chance like this for ages!"

"No. It's too dangerous. I can't let you do it. There are scores of underlings I could send to take care of this errand," he said with calculation.

"I only want to help out my 'daddy,' " she said in her most girlish and wheedling voice. Then, in English, she said, "I'll try my best!" She continued in Japanese: "I'll give it everything I have!"

"Well, my dear. Not only do you have a genius for espio-nage, you also have quite a talent for languages. I haven't mis-judged you!" he said, praising her to the skies. She really was fearless, he thought.

Uno stepped around so that he stood facing her and looked directly into her eyes.

"If I ever lost you, Yoshiko, I would be like a samurai who had lost his sword."

"Hey!" she said, shaking him. "Isn't that pouring it on a bit thick? Tell your scriptwriter to tone it down a little, all right?"

"I only want to make you happy."

Still sitting on her barstool, Yoshiko reached out and encircled his waist with her arms. She raised her head just far enough to meet his eyes and stayed that way for quite some time, gazing at him provocatively. Suddenly, she gave him a tight squeeze and buried her head between his legs, but his military trousers blocked her progress. She closed her eyes and chanted seductively in a low and sleepy voice.

"I thought it was the woman's duty to do everything she could to make her man happy."

The world outside was pitch-black and deathly still, but this hotel bar, with its blazing lanterns, was an island of warmth and light. The blank-faced darkness pressed in on all sides, but the lounge was like an enormous, cozy bed.

Yoshiko unfastened the buttons of Uno's trousers. Then she took hold of the zipper with her fine white teeth and slowly drew it down. Slyly, she gave him a light bite, and he responded. . . .

It was a very, very long night.

While she was living in Port Arthur, Yoshiko had a chance to meet some of her younger brothers and sisters for the first time. They were not yet born when she was sent away to Japan, and they had grown up in her absence.

Try as she might, she was unable to win their affection. Sadly, she had become a foreigner in their eyes. They were outwardly polite toward her, but the older brothers and sisters advised the younger ones not to get too close to her. Her improper escapades attracted too much attention, and her flamboyant political activities bore the taint of scandal. Her elder siblings regarded her as an immoral and abnormal woman, and they warned the others off in no uncertain terms. When, on the tenth anniversary of her father's death, a memorial plaque was erected in the garden of his residence, Yoshiko was not invited to the ceremony.

But she had her own life to live. She would put on a cropped fur coat, tight skirt, high heels, and lots of heavy makeup, and go for a stroll downtown. She cut quite a flashy figure in this outfit, and she turned a lot of heads.

There was gossip about her liaisons with certain Japanese men, and it wasn't long before her elder brothers sent the younger sisters away to school in Japan. They wanted those impressionable girls to be as far away from Yoshiko as possible.

Deeply hurt, Yoshiko immersed herself in her work. She was determined not to become like the other members of Prince Su's family, reduced to living like commoners! It took great men and women to change the world. Fate never helped anyone who didn't help himself!

Her brothers and sisters were her own flesh and blood. Why, she even shared a mother with some of them. And they all had the same father. She was part of their family, and yet they felt nothing for her, as though she weren't good enough for them. She was an outsider, but was it she who was the odd one? No! The truth was that she was the only one of them who had any potential at all!

The burden fell on her to make things happen and get results. To fail would be to betray her father's faith in her, and render those long years he labored meaningless. She couldn't let that happen. She had a great opportunity before her. She couldn't fail.

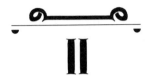

II

Tientsin. The Garden of Tranquillity, Pu-yi's villa, was located on Harmony and Prosperity Lane in the Japanese concession of Tientsin. The plaque on its outer wall read CHING COURT OFFICE—TIENTSIN BRANCH, for when Pu-yi had named this villa "The Garden of Tranquillity," he had not been seeking the tranquillity of a peaceful retirement. A more accurate reading of his intentions would have been: Watch and wait.

When its master was at home, the villa had been a miniature Forbidden City. The emperor's old retainers insisted on referring to it as a "temporary residence," as though the emperor were only staying there because some business had briefly taken him away from Peking. Loyal "subjects" came to the villa to pay their respects, and others managed the affairs of this shrunken domain, where the old Ching calendar was still observed and where the emperor and empress were treated according to the strictest rules of court etiquette.

One day, after the emperor's departure from Tientsin, a small sedan drove up to the imposing main gate of the Garden of Tranquillity. The car sat idling for a moment.

There were all kinds of people in the road in front of the gate—hawkers, passersby, drivers—an ordinary and harmless mix, at least on the surface. In fact, there was probably more to some of them than met the eye, but it would have taken an expert to tell for sure who was a plainclothes policeman and who was genuine.

The rather forbidding guards who stood watch inside the gate observed an aristocratic lady in a black fur-lined cloak and high heels stepping out of the car. Under the cloak, she wore a deep, rich red cheongsam, embroidered with a pattern of dragons in silver and gold threads.

Accompanying this lady was an elegant gentleman in a European suit of the finest English wool—the sort of thing that could only be found in first-class foreign department stores like Harrods. A pair of diamond cuff links and a matching tie tack completed his outfit.

This beautifully turned-out couple was there to call on the residents of the Garden of Tranquillity. The man followed the woman up to the gate, where the gatekeeper looked them over once or twice before beckoning them in with a smile. The woman's imported perfume lingered in the air outside the gate long after she entered the compound. The two were not what they appeared to be, for she was Yoshiko Kawashima, and her "husband" was her handpicked assistant, Young Lin.

Young Lin felt greatly honored that Yoshiko had chosen to

include him in such an important operation, and he was determined to do his job well. Before they left for Tientsin, Yoshiko had commanded Young Lin to spend an evening out on the town with her. "All work and no play makes you a very dull boy," she teased him. They did go out dancing together, and it was rumored that Young Lin spent the night with her, although no one will ever know.

They waited for some time before they were admitted to the empress Wan-jung's boudoir.

Yoshiko was shocked by what she saw. Lying on the bed was a sallow-faced woman with sunken eyes and blackened teeth, smoking opium. All of her movements were tremendously slow. She took a long draw on her opium pipe, closed her eyes, and let out a contented sigh, afloat in the drug's euphoric haze. Was this woman really the empress?

She looked up lazily at the visitor standing before her bed and regarded her with heavy-lidded eyes. She knew why these visitors had come.

"Best wishes to Her Majesty the empress!" Yoshiko said formally. "We've brought you a little treat, your favorite."

Yoshiko took out a finely wrought metal box. When she slid the top open just a crack, the sweet scent of high-grade opium filled the air.

"I remembered that you liked this kind in particular. I've heard that it's difficult to get here in Tientsin."

"I have no intention of leaving Tientsin," Wan-jung said coldly.

"The emperor misses you. He's worried about you."

"Ha!" she spat. "If only I were like Wen-hsiu. She got a divorce. But can I get a divorce? No! I'm the empress, and empresses don't do things like that."

She was very agitated and blinked angrily, but her mood

changed abruptly, and she began to whimper.

"It's dragging me down—it's killing me. I can never go back, never be an ordinary person again!"

Yoshiko saw her chance and sat down on the edge of the bed.

"Whenever I see you, you always seem so unhappy," she said solicitously, drawing closer.

"It's not that I'm unhappy," Wan-jung complained. "It's just that I never feel safe. My husband is the emperor—yet he can do absolutely nothing to protect me!"

She was growing hysterical, trapped in the tangled net of her own emotions. Her life was already half over, and here she was, a lonely, helpless, abandoned woman. She felt as though she were surrounded on all sides by curtains of flame. There was no way out.

"I might as well be dead!" she screamed. "There's nothing I can do anymore! Just leave me alone and let me live out what's left of this miserable life in peace!" She began crying uncontrollably, like a madwoman. Her shoulders trembled violently as tears of pain and despair streamed down her cheeks. Before anyone realized what was happening, Wan-jung knocked over her opium lamp, and within an instant the bed canopy had caught fire.

Without a moment's hesitation, Yoshiko picked up a pillow and smothered the little flame. She was a picture of complete calm, for the only thing going through her mind at that moment was that it was a perfect opportunity.

Looking in through the hole that had been burned in the canopy, Yoshiko saw the empress clearly. She was a pathetic excuse for an empress, to be sure, as she sat shaking and gasping for air like a small, frightened animal.

Yoshiko regarded her coolly. Wan-jung wore an utterly

defeated expression, and her eyes were still full of tears.

"I have no one! No one!" she mumbled to herself. "Just give me some poison to drink!"

Cautiously, Yoshiko approached her and slowly wrapped her up in the black fur-lined cape. The fur was thick and soft, and it still held the warmth of Yoshiko's body. An empress in name only, Wan-jung was really just a frail and helpless woman.

How much stronger I am than you! Yoshiko thought to herself.

"I'm right here. I won't let anything happen to you," she said, as though comforting a small child. "Be a good girl and don't cry! I'll take you somewhere very safe—to Shanghai. We'll have a good time there. How would that be? Shanghai is a wonderful place. And nobody will be spying on you day and night. Everyone there is a good friend. People there are trustworthy."

Wan-jung rested her head on Yoshiko's breast.

"Every day, when I wake up," she murmured softly, "I feel as though there were fifty or sixty people watching my every move. They're like demons sent from hell, always watching. When it gets dark in the palace at night, I get so terrified I break into a cold sweat. Please! Take me away from here!"

She clung to Yoshiko like a weak vine clinging to the safety of a firm stone wall. She had nowhere else to turn.

Wan-jung was still for a moment, and Yoshiko waited patiently. When Wan-jung stirred, it was to pull off her jade earrings; she gently fastened them onto Yoshiko's ears. Wan-jung thought Yoshiko's earlobes were especially beautiful now, with flashes of bright green jade dangling from them.

An imperceptible sneer of contempt flickered briefly at the corner of Yoshiko's mouth, but her voice was warm and soothing.

"Go ahead. Touch them," she said.

"They're cold," Wan-jung said, smiling.

Yoshiko firmly took hold of Wan-jung's hand and pressed it to her earlobe so hard that the earring cut into Wan-jung's hand. Unperturbed, Wan-jung felt her eyelids grow heavy, for she was on the verge of surrendering to a deep sleep. She felt completely safe. Her troubles were over, and this was the most warm and protected place in all the world.

Yoshiko glanced down at her. She was so naive, such a trusting little creature.

"Just do as I say, and everything will be fine," Yoshiko instructed and, drawing Wan-jung closer, she held her tight and kissed her gently.

Wan-jung felt a strangely seductive dizziness come over her. Languidly, she closed her eyes, and her arms went limp.

Yoshiko's kisses became more forceful, more urgent. . . .

Afterward, Wan-jung trusted Yoshiko completely, so Yoshiko's plan went into effect the next day. As Yoshiko directed, Wan-jung went to Yoshiko's guest room, where she saw that the carpet by the bed was soiled with vomit. Young Lin, Yoshiko's "husband," was lying on the bed, feigning the listlessness of an invalid. There were traces of blood at the corners of his mouth.

"My husband and I are grateful for Her Majesty's kind concern," Yoshiko declaimed in a loud, clear voice, for she intended that others in the house would hear. The Garden of Tranquillity was a den of intrigues and petty plots, where none of the staff were entirely above suspicion, and some of them were probably plainclothes policemen. The drama she was performing had to be convincing, and Yoshiko played the part of the caring wife to the hilt, rushing in and out of the sickroom and anxiously reporting her husband's condition to the maidservant.

"I'm afraid that my husband just isn't accustomed to the climate here. It seems to have caused an old stomach ailment of his to flare up. Perhaps I could trouble you to arrange for an ambulance to take him to the hospital."

While Yoshiko was in the hall, putting this final touch on the cover story, Young Lin and Wan-jung hurriedly exchanged clothing in the guest room. Young Lin did his best to maintain professional decorum.

"Please forgive any improprieties, Majesty," he whispered respectfully to the empress.

Yoshiko gave one final order to the maid before returning to the guest room.

"I'm going to help him dress. Inform me the instant the ambulance arrives!"

Next came the most critical part of the drama that Yoshiko was directing and performing for Wan-jung's nosy staff. What they saw as they watched from a discreet distance was an effusively apologetic Yoshiko accompanying the empress back to her bedchamber.

"Please accept my humblest and most abject apologies, Majesty. I am so ashamed—Your Majesty has been so kind to favor us with an audience, yet we have been nothing but trouble! Please forgive us!"

The two went inside the empress's room, and Yoshiko shut the door behind them. They were offstage, and Yoshiko turned around to face Young Lin—for it was not the empress at all, but Young Lin disguised in her clothes. He went over to the bed and lay down.

"You don't need to worry about me, Miss Yoshiko," he said. "I'll be fine on my own. After it's dark, I can find my way out of here."

Yoshiko had played her part well, but now the first act of

the play was over. She regarded Young Lin with detachment. Her face was as cold and hard as the moon.

And the gun was already in her hand.

Young Lin was dumbstruck and half rose from the bed, but he went numb with shock as icy fear crept from his toes to his head. Even his thoughts were paralyzed. Before he had time to wonder what was happening, Yoshiko placed a pillow over his chest to muffle the sound of the shot and fired the gun into it. He died instantly.

Yoshiko had no intention of leaving any witnesses behind. This operation was hers—the risk was hers, and the credit would be hers, as well. She would stop at nothing in order to protect the security of this mission.

She tidied up a bit. Blood was welling up through the pillow and spreading a bright red stain across the snow-white pillowcase. She drew the quilt up over Young Lin's still-warm body.

"What a shame! Such a handsome boy!" she said in farewell.

Yoshiko stepped into the hall outside the bedchamber, and her face was instantly masked in worry. She hurried downstairs.

"Has the ambulance come yet?" she pressed the servants.

As she spoke, an ambulance drew up and stopped in front of the main gate, and a pair of white-coated medics rushed into the house with a stretcher. They were quick, for in no time at all they emerged from the house and carefully bore the invalid to the waiting car. The turned up collar of the patient's overcoat, and the muffler wrapped around the head obscured the patient's face. The sound of labored breathing came from the inert form. Yoshiko was a perfect picture of concern and distress as she followed her "sick husband" out to the ambulance and climbed in beside him, fussing over him all the way.

They drove away from the Garden of Tranquillity, but even with the villa behind them, they were still not entirely safe. Although they were on the relatively secure soil of the Japanese concession, they still had to worry about spies and assassins.

Wan-jung was too afraid to move. She had entrusted herself to Yoshiko, and she held on to Yoshiko's hand as tightly as if her life depended on it.

The ambulance, of course, was also part of Yoshiko's plan. As the vehicle sped smoothly onward, Yoshiko looked out the window, her eyes riveted on the street. When they came to the barricades at certain intersections, she surreptitiously gave a signal, and they were allowed to pass without stopping.

Once they were outside the Japanese concession, Yoshiko's expression grew even harder.

"Where will we stay in Shanghai?" Wan-jung asked.

"We're going to Manchuria," Yoshiko replied flatly.

"Manchuria!" Wan-jung exclaimed in shock and disbelief. "Am I still going to be ordered around by the Japanese?"

Yoshiko said nothing.

"I won't go!" Wan-jung was becoming frantic. "Why did you trick me? Why are you making me go to Manchuria? Isn't the emperor just a prisoner there?"

"You are the empress. You have your duty!"

Wan-jung looked at Yoshiko and saw how tough and capable she was, how unlike herself.

"And what is that duty?" Wan-jung asked suspiciously. She half rose, but Yoshiko pushed her down firmly.

"The emperor is to be crowned in Changchun, and you will be there, by his side. That's where you belong, and where you shall remain until the day you die!"

Wan-jung struggled to break free. She had fallen from one trap right into another.

"I won't go!" she protested loudly. "I don't trust you! You—"

But she did not finish what she was saying. Yoshiko placed a chloroform-soaked handkerchief over her mouth, and she lapsed into unconsciousness.

Yoshiko stared straight ahead, her eyes unwavering and her face devoid of emotion, as the ambulance drove out of the city and then headed into the open countryside. Its destination was an obscure hamlet.

Back in Tientsin, the calm of the Garden of Tranquillity was broken. Young Lin's body was discovered, and several unmarked cars were sent in hot pursuit of the mysterious ambulance. But Yoshiko expected this to happen and was well prepared.

The ambulance reached the hamlet and stopped at an isolated cottage. Yoshiko got out, managing, with some difficulty, to half lift and half drag Wan-jung's limp, unconscious form out of the back of the car.

Waiting behind the cottage, at the foot of a small hill, was a funeral party. They stood in patient silence around an empty coffin. They were waiting for Wan-jung, and now that she had arrived, they wordlessly carried her to the coffin and placed her inside. Then the ambulance was driven into a ditch and camouflaged with twigs and leafy branches. At the same time, Yoshiko quickly changed her costume and transformed herself into a simple peasant woman with a tear-streaked face. It all took less than five minutes.

The pallbearers put the lid on the coffin and raised it up onto their shoulders. An old man led off the procession, scattering paper spirit money on the ground as he went. Horns and drums struck up a dirge, and the rest of the party—filial sons, friends, and family—set off down the road weeping and wailing loudly.

As the procession snaked slowly along the country road, a pair of unmarked pursuit cars came whizzing by, scraping past the rustic band of mourners. There was nothing about these solemn peasants to arouse even the slightest suspicion among the pursuers.

Yoshiko's group made its way back to Tientsin. From there, Wan-jung was taken by boat up to Port Arthur. The operation was conducted in complete secrecy, and Yoshiko's plan came off without a hitch. She had made her mark.

12

The Japanese were an unstoppable force: Their power was on the rise, and their arrogance knew no bounds. The emperor and empress were together again, and the half-million square miles of territory and 30 million inhabitants of Manchuria were under Japanese control. The Japanese were right where they wanted to be.

Pu-yi began to feel uneasy—something didn't seem quite right. He, the empress, and their entourage were kept in isolation, their movements dictated by their Japanese masters. Most disturbing of all was a remark made by the Kwantung Army staff officer Seishiro Itagaki, a squat man with a shaved head and a stony, gray face.

"The new nation shall be called Manchukuo," he drawled. "The capital will be in Changchun, which will be renamed Hsinching, or 'New Capital.' Five races—Manchu, Chinese, Mongolian, Japanese, and Korean—will share this new nation. However, since the Japanese people have, over the past several decades, made many sacrifices for this land, in many cases laying down their lives, it is only natural that they be given special consideration. Namely, that their legal and political positions should be different from those of other races. . . ."

Pu-yi found this disconcerting, but the question that troubled him most was this: Were they going to let him be emperor again, or were they merely going to allow him to be the "ruler" of Manchukuo? True, many innocent people had been slaughtered in Manchuria, and Japan had long schemed to colonize the territory. But these matters, along with the questions of how many soldiers Japan would send, how much ore the Japanese would mine, and how much oil, salt, and grain they would cart off—these were all matters of indifference to Pu-yi. Only one question was close to his heart, and it consumed all of his attention: Would he be emperor again? His life would be meaningless if he couldn't be emperor. The old retainers, many of them men in their eighties, who crowded around him appealed to him tearily: It was his sacred duty to serve as emperor, and it was their sacred duty to see that he did so.

Negotiations dragged on. Careful not to expose the extent of their ambition, the Japanese referred to the time as a "Period of Transition" and promised to install Pu-yi in a year. In the end, they did grant him the title of emperor, but he was an emperor in name only. Nonetheless, the title was enough to satisfy Pu-yi, who willingly ceded any real power and endured the humiliation of being a puppet. The Kwantung Army made his dreams of imperial splendor come true, and he did not dare reproach its leaders for slaughtering countless numbers of his countrymen. He was fearful of offending them.

Pu-yi's perseverance paid off on March 1, 1934, when he at last became emperor again. Pu-yi and the Japanese haggled until the last minute over one last point: the question of Pu-yi's attire. He insisted on wearing a Ching emperor's traditional dragon-embroidered robes, but a commanding officer in the Kwantung Army informed him that this was out of the question: Japan was permitting Pu-yi to be emperor of Manchukuo, not of the Ching dynasty! They demanded that he wear the uniform of the commander in chief of the armed forces. But this was one compromise Pu-yi declined to make, and he refused to back down. He wanted to don the robes of a Ching emperor and hear his loyal subjects shout, "Long live the emperor!" The tug-of-war over Pu-yi's costume dragged on and on.

The day of Pu-yi's coronation arrived. He mounted the high circular platform, erected only that morning and meant to stand in for the Temple of Heaven in Peking, brimming with self-satisfaction. He was wearing the dragon robes—he had won! Someone had to rush off to Peking at the last minute to get this costume from his late father's consort, Jung-hui. It was said that these robes had once been worn by Pu-yi's predecessor as emperor of China, Kuang-hsu. The empress was also splendidly arrayed in a brocade robe and a crown decorated with thirteen phoenixes, the traditional symbol of the empress. The old Ching loyalists also dug up their old ceremonial court dress. They wore coral-beaded caps with trailing pheasant feathers and the coats with crane or golden pheasant appliqués—insignia of rank—and long strings of ceremonial beads. Many of them had lost their original strings of precious or semiprecious stones and wore strings of abacus beads instead.

A band struck up the Manchurian national anthem. The sky

was overcast, and an icy wind cut through the assembly. Still, nothing could dampen the spirits of the gathered Manchu officials as they watched the emperor reverently performing the ancient rituals of kneeling and kowtowing to heaven. Squeezed between two rows of Japanese rising suns were the eight banners of the eight clans of the once-mighty Ching. The emperor's own standard-bearers, holding aloft yellow dragon pennants, knelt for the entire ceremony. Pu-yi was so moved by these solemn proceedings that his eyes brimmed with tears.

Yoshiko was there, too. She was one of the people who had made this event possible, she thought smugly. Her heart beat proudly in her breast, and she was filled with inexpressible excitement as she watched the emperor of the mighty Ching being restored to his rightful position.

Manchukuo has been born at last! she thought to herself. We had to wait for twenty years, but now that we've started, nothing will be able to stop us. Manchukuo is just the beginning—someday all of China will be returned to us, and the Ching Empire shall reign once more! And with the rebirth of the empire will come the destruction of all those who helped to overthrow it. They will be made to pay!

These thoughts crowded her head as she proudly watched the awe-inspiring and sacred ritual. Every sacrifice she had made was worth it.

She recalled a poem her father, Prince Su, wrote when he was forced to leave Peking:

The wild goose wings home to his native land,
He cries out in sorrow on his flight northeast.
Looking back, he sees the fires of war behind him,
As the sun sets red over the plains of China.

Yoshiko would always remember this day as the most glorious day of her life. Dressed in military uniform, with jodhpurs, leather boots, and an army cap, she looked very fine indeed. An ornately wrought sword hung from her waist on gold braid, and two guns nestled in leather holsters—a brand-new "type two" Mauser and a Carter automatic pistol. Her shiny polished boots clicked sharply with every footstep as she stepped up to the rostrum, radiating confidence. Shunkichi Uno, her patron, protector, lover, and boss, pinned a three-star medal of honor onto her shoulder and bestowed on her a new title: Commander Chin Pi-hui of the Pacification Army of Manchukuo.

There were five thousand troops under her command, and her rank of commander in chief entitled her to an official seal one inch square. This gave her the authority to issue orders. Many men opposed to the Manchus and Japanese would submit happily to the authority of this charismatic princess. Yoshiko, now called Commander Chin, was a legend, something especially amazing for one so young, and she reveled in her newfound fame. For their part, the Japanese were happy to indulge her fantasy by flattering her. Although she thought she was using them to achieve her own ends, it was they who were using her; but she was too intoxicated by everything to see that.

The Japanese were the masters of Manchukuo, and since they mistrusted other races, they sought to dominate all aspects of life—politics, economics, ideology, and culture. They pretended to promote what they called "Coexistence and Coprosperity," but all this slogan really meant was "Be like us." Japanese became a required course in elementary and middle schools, and official documents were written in Japanese, not Manchu or Chinese. Japanese people were first-class citizens, and city planners renamed the streets of the new capital after the streets of Japan's old capitals of Kyoto and Nara.

The coronation was an international affair, with guests attired in everything from kimonos to Western suits to Chinese clothes. There were the heads of the corporations that controlled or produced all of life's necessities—railroads, heavy industry, coal mining, utilities, telephone and telegraph, gold mining, aviation, and agriculture. There were military officers, tycoons, artists, writers, musicians, and reporters. Flashbulbs were popping nonstop, and in the midst of this dazzling swirl of activity, there was Yoshiko. She wore a proud and haughty expression, but the suggestion of a bewitching smile played about her lips as she lifted her chin slightly every time she shook hands.

Sometime later one of the guests passed forward a card announcing the arrival of yet another guest, who bore the rather outlandish title of "Army Major and China Group Head, Bureau of Information, Division of Pacification, North China Expeditionary Force Headquarters." Yoshiko's eyes immediately went to the man's name: Yamaga.

Yamaga? Yoshiko raised her eyes and took a look around. She couldn't believe it—it was him! Had he been transferred to Manchuria?

He had put on a little weight in the intervening years. He must be going on forty, she thought to herself. Dignity had come with age, and the cocky young upstart was gone, replaced by a man who appeared to be a quintessentially old-fashioned intellectual. He had a slightly eccentric but elegant demeanor, and was clad in a full-length Chinese scholar's robe and a felt cap. A beautifully carved walking stick completed the picture. His Mandarin Chinese was perfect, of course, since she was the one who'd taught it to him.

A flood of memories surged over Yoshiko, mingled with a trace of regret. She was not the girl she used to be—and he had changed, too. There was no going back—that was the saddest thing about life. The welter of conflicting emotions made her senses reel, but Yamaga seemed unruffled.

"How do you do, Commander Chin," he said coolly.

Despising him for being able to act as though there had never been anything between them, she gave an even colder response.

"Thank you for coming. Your presence is appreciated."

He undoubtedly knew all about her, including who was responsible for her new title of "Commander Chin." Was that why he mocked her?

I'll show you that I'm a good woman! she'd once told him; but now these words came back to mock her. Shame turned to anger, and she left the reception shortly after, determined to put him, and all that he reminded her of, far behind her. She leapt onto the back of a fast horse and galloped over the open country around Hsinching. When she was high up in the saddle, astride her tall stallion, no one could touch her. Surveying the world from her lofty perch, she felt above everyone. She was incomparable!

So what if she was evil and would stop at nothing as she clawed her way to the top! There was no going back, now. She banished Yamaga, and everybody else, from her mind. She was above them all.

13

Yoshiko was back in Shanghai, a place she loved, the place where she first made a name for herself. The situation in Manchukuo was developing according to Japanese plans, but Japan was still worried about possible opposition from the League of Nations. For this reason, Uno sent Yoshiko back to Shanghai on another important mission—the task of instigating the events that later became known as the Shanghai Incident.

Anti-Japanese sentiment among the citizens of Shanghai was seething just beneath the surface, and underground resistance organizations proliferated. Yoshiko bribed a worker at the Mitsutomo Company's towel factory to lead a raid against the monks of the Japanese Buddhist Sanmyo Temple. There were casualties.

Next, she incited a group of some thirty Japanese monks to go to the factory and seek reprisals. What started as a dispute between a few individuals gained size and momentum until, in the end, the factory was burned to the ground, a thousand workers were killed or injured, and a supposed hotbed of anti-Japanese feeling was dealt a harsh blow. International attention was focused on Shanghai as China and Japan faced off, and the eyes of the world were distracted from Japan's consolidation of territory in the Northeast. Meanwhile, Japan launched a military invasion in the South. Yoshiko thought herself very clever, exempt from the dangers of these troubled times, a perfect spy.

In Shanghai, Yoshiko shed her military uniform and once again became the graceful dancer who charmed the city. Night after night, she went out, abandoning herself to the pleasures of Shanghai's nightlife. Youthful, excited blood coursed through her veins—it seemed she couldn't stop dancing. But throughout those days and nights, with their endless rounds of drinking and dancing and endless strings of parties and dance partners, she was hard at work gathering valuable information from those same men whose company seemed to delight her so.

She learned many things. The Nineteenth Route Army was fighting in isolation. Chiang Kai-shek was on the verge of retiring. She knew who was steadfast in his resistance to Japan; whose allegiance could be bought; who was a counterspy. Nationalist China's Kuomintang-controlled banks were on the brink of collapse. China desired a cease-fire. These rumors and many like them were channeled through Yoshiko to her bosses. The Japanese had only to send this one girl to do their bidding, and their investment came back tenfold.

Yoshiko wondered at times if she were just a Japanese errand girl, serving their interests; but she persuaded herself that her interests and those of Japan were identical. She didn't have to make excuses to anyone!

With her mastery of both Chinese and Japanese, she moved freely between those two worlds; and she changed guises just as freely, slipping from European dresses to kimonos to cheongsams to slinky evening gowns that trailed the ground. Sometimes she was a woman, sometimes a man. It was this fact of her persona that Japanese officers found especially seductive. These veterans of many long years of warfare counted men as well as women among their conquests. Yoshiko reminded them of one of the Kabuki actors who portray female characters onstage—every Japanese man's secret ideal. Ever so subtly, they were aroused by her.

Men who had never seen her were so intrigued by the wild tales of "Venus in a Suit" that they ached with the desire just to catch a glimpse of her. Because of the intensity of this desire, those who met her tended to fall easily under her spell. Men flocked to her, and her circle of contacts grew ever wider. She might turn up among the spectators at the annual sumo championships at Tokyo's National Stadium; or, dressed in a tasteful and costly pale pink kimono, on the arm of a general. She might be seen on the second floor of the Shiseido Building in the Ginza, holding hands and sipping tea with a millionaire businessman. At other times, Yoshiko was spotted cruising around Shanghai in a flashy sedan, clad in a man's brown suit and overcoat, a beret rakishly tipped to one side.

A coterie of tall, strapping young men waited on her hand and foot in her luxurious mansion. They claimed to be her bodyguards, but they served her more intimately. She no longer cared what anybody thought, and she did as she pleased, not even bothering to get out of bed before one or two in the afternoon. She lolled around in silk pajamas, conducting all manner of business from her boudoir.

One day a handsome young fellow, smartly turned-out in a suit and hat, came to call. It was an honor to have a personal audience with Yoshiko.

"The job's finished," she said, handing him a photograph. "This particular agent provocateur is of no use to us anymore."

"Yes, ma'am," he said, backing toward the door and bowing repeatedly.

"Report to me at the theater in several days' time."

"I'll see to it myself, Commander Chin!"

"Good. By the way, my patron, Mr. Uno, is out of town right now. Why don't you come out dancing with me tomorrow night?"

"Yes, ma'am!" he replied, and went out.

Outside of Yoshiko's room, the young man ran into Yoshiko's personal secretary, Chizuko, a young Japanese woman who saw to every detail of Yoshiko's life with care and devotion. She was accustomed to her mistress's wild behavior, and she didn't even bat an eye anymore. She had a report to make to Yoshiko.

"Miss Yoshiko, I have completed a detailed account of Mr. Yamaga's activities since his arrival here in Shanghai."

Yoshiko looked up.

"Put on Beethoven's *Moonlight Sonata* for me first."

The notes floated lightly up, filling the room, and Yoshiko gave a long stretch. She felt as though she were entering a dreamworld, where moonlight glimmered through the melody and sprinkled down onto her body ever so lightly, covering her in moonbeams.

What had he been up to these past few days? Where had he gone? Whom had he seen? Was he happy? Was he depressed?

The thrill of spying on her former lover gave her butterflies, but none of this excitement showed in her voice.

"All right. You may proceed," she directed Chizuko.

Chizuko began:

Yamaga was depressed for a while after an unhappy love affair, but later he went to Peking and took up cultural propaganda work along with a Chinese name, Wang Chia-heng. In 1930, he married Kiyoko, the only daughter of a reporter, in Peking, and three years later Kiyoko gave birth to a daughter, Hiroko. With the founding of Manchukuo, Yamaga was transferred to the Northeast, where he was put in charge of propaganda and published a newspaper, organized a theater troupe, and produced other performing-arts events. He was a man of some power and influence, with mansions in Hsinching, Peking, Shanghai, and Tientsin. Recently, he had been busy preparing to set up a film studio in Manchukuo, the purpose of which was to further spread pro-Japanese propaganda in the region, and he went around searching for "suitable" young women whom he could turn into stars. But he was just a front man. The real power behind the scenes was Lieutenant Masahiko Amakasu.

Yamaga's work brought him into contact with an extravagant crowd of movie people and bohemians. He went with a fast crowd and lived high, and had a reputation as a womanizer. A bevy of starlets, all craving fame and fortune, vied for his attention, affectionately addressing him as "Daddy Wang."

Starlets. Affairs. Power. "International Friendship."

Chizuko continued her report, but Yoshiko heard nothing but a long string of women's names, twisting and turning, snaking around her mind—Li Li-hua, Chen Yun-shang, Chou Manhua, Chen Yen-yen—which was which? They all sounded alike. Which ones had he actually slept with?

Yamaga had followed her advice and pulled himself together after all. A part of her had wanted to see him stumble and fall, spiritually and physically, because of her. Instead, he got back on his feet and became a great success! Gripped by a deep-seated jealousy, Yoshiko tightened her jaw.

"That will be all," she told Chizuko sweetly.

The record played on, stubbornly spinning around and around, filling the room with a sickly-sweet romanticism that hemmed her in with her anger. But didn't she have affairs, too?

In the throes of passion, she always moaned, "Leave it alone. Nobody touches that. Nobody." She jealously guarded her left breast and its secret.

Men would hold her tight; and she seemed so delicate and vulnerable.

"Is it because your heart is on the left side?" some would wonder.

"Is there a scar from your old wound?"

Each had his own theory, and each wanted to know why, but she restrained their curious hands, saying:

"You mustn't!"

If they used just a little force, they could overpower her, and then they would see it: a tiny red mole on her left breast. It winked temptingly in the flickering lamplight, its unattainability exciting them further. They mounted her ecstatically, drunkenly, madly, using their hands, their tongues, and even their teeth to try to excite this mark of her beauty.

But her charms were more than skin-deep, and a night spent with her was something no man could ever forget. Still, she saved this one tiny part of herself. Was she saving it for Yamaga?

He no longer cared a bit for her!

Yoshiko looked pallid but wrote it off as just a lack of sleep.

One night shortly afterward, Yamaga had gone out with a beautiful young Shanghainese actress. He brought her home, and they embraced, kissing passionately in the dark outside his mansion. Locked in this tight embrace, he still somehow managed to open the door with a free hand and switch on the light. The couple's eyes met with a shocking scene. The house was in total disarray—everything they saw was shattered, ripped, or otherwise broken to pieces. Bits of torn-up photographs were strewn about—mostly photos of Yamaga and various starlets—among shredded love letters addressed to "Daddy Wang," smashed cameras, shattered vases, and broken glass. Ruined clothing littered the floor—suits, kimonos, and even his undershirts and shorts, all ripped to shreds. Nothing had been spared. Not one thing in the entire house was left whole.

Yamaga and his companion were agape, but an even bigger shock still awaited them. In the midst of this devastation, sitting on the sofa as though it were her own, was Yoshiko Kawashima. With her feet up and her arms draped across the back of the couch, she gazed at them disdainfully. The arrogant curl of her lip told them that she had been waiting for quite some time.

14

With great delicacy and tact, Yamaga eased his companion out the front door.

"Why don't you run along home now? I'll phone you first thing in the morning!"

The frightened young woman had no desire to stay and left in a hurry.

Once rid of his date, Yamaga shut the door and turned to face Yoshiko. For some time, neither of them spoke as they traded blank stares. Yoshiko made no move to apologize.

"You really get around, don't you?" she said frostily. "Whether you're at work or at play, there must be plenty of lovely ladies just throwing themselves at you, some of them quite openly, I'll bet!"

"It's usually work and not play," he replied.

"Giving those starlets acting lessons, are you? Helping them practice their love scenes?"

With great effort, Yamaga checked his temper. "That's my business!"

"The girls you like are all Chinese," she said provocatively. He didn't respond.

Suddenly, she shouted at him:

"Why don't you like Japanese girls?"

He remained silent. Tension filled the air. In that brief moment, their thoughts traveled over a thousand miles and back, and both were filled with confusion. Why didn't he like Japanese girls?

She sneered.

"Maybe it's because *I'm* a Chinese girl," she said smugly.

Yamaga listened, feeling torn. He was getting old, and he hadn't risen as far or as fast as he'd hoped. He wasted his youth on his career, and for what? He was middle-aged, and had found neither professional success nor true love. He was just a cog in a wheel.

He chuckled ironically.

"You have much too high an opinion of yourself, Commander Chin!"

Gesturing toward the door, as though to usher her out, he added:

"It's late. Please go."

These weren't the words Yoshiko wanted to hear, and she ignored his request. Instead, she threw herself at him, clinging tight, and resisting when he pushed her away in disgust. She wasn't about to let him get away with this. She always got what she wanted—all it took was a little effort. Like the vortex of a whirlpool, she drew in the object of her desire with sheer force of will, until it rested in the palm of her hand. No man could evade her once she set her sights on him, and this fact gave her immense satisfaction. She thrived on this success—it made her beautiful.

She wasn't about to let him slip away. In an instant, her face changed. Who in all the world understood him best? She lightly and lovingly caressed his weathered face.

"Were any of them even half as good as I?" she purred. "Hm? Tell me."

Bit by bit, nostalgia crept over him. She embraced him tightly, offering him her red lips and covering his mouth with hers, so that he could not speak. He was powerless to resist. Once, he believed she would be his. She would make him sweet date-filled rice cakes every day for the rest of his life. But that was a long time ago. . . .

His hand moved around from her back to her breasts, and she felt a shock go through her body. With their bodies pressed tightly together as though one, they did not move for a long time. When at last he began to stir, she wrapped herself around him like a serpent, whetting his appetite, showing him how lucky he was to be with her. None of the other women he'd had could compare.

She took her time, giving him pleasure beyond his wildest dreams, making him so happy he could die. She suckled him hungrily. Men had taught her to do this, and she learned well. Experienced and confident in her ability to give and receive pleasure, she found that fate had brought her back to her first love. But she now felt slightly contemptuous of him.

Suddenly, and without warning, Yoshiko turned on him, biting down as hard as she could on his mouth. He cried out in pain through bleeding tongue and lips.

Yamaga then stared at her blankly and wiped the sweet,

sticky blood from his mouth with the back of his hand. It was surprisingly painful. He eyed Yoshiko steadily, this baffling she-devil.

She threw her head back and laughed lightheartedly, then pushed him away with disgust, just as he had pushed her away only a little while before. Although she was uninjured, there was a streak of blood on her face—his blood, looking like smeared lipstick beside her crimson-painted mouth. She sprawled, naked, and laughed wantonly.

"I'm not anybody's good little girl!" she said with a wicked smile. "It may be over between us, but you were my first love, and I will always have a claim on you. I can't simply stand by while you do as you please. I won't let you get away with it! Don't underestimate me!" she added menacingly.

She rose and stepped into the moonlight and put her clothing back on, one piece at a time, all the while facing him. It was as though she were building a wall, brick by brick, cutting herself off from him. Yamaga felt completely off balance. Only moments before, he had been lost in an indescribable ecstasy—then in an instant it was gone.

Yoshiko swished out of the room, and he stared mutely at her retreating back. A big, fat drop of blood welled out of his torn lips. He was alone with his thoughts. In China on a mission of national importance, he considered himself a man of bold ambition. He was central to the efforts to ensure that the newly born state of Manchukuo would be filled with "pure" and unswervingly loyal cultural influences, and had the important task of setting up a Manchurian film studio. As head of this enterprise, he was constantly surrounded with attractive women, all preening and tittering like so many brightly colored birds. He used them, and they used him—so what? Somehow, though, he provoked the ire of this particular woman.

Who knew what nasty tricks she might play on him later on? She was capable of anything. Yamaga sat down wearily, weighed down by his worries, and stayed that way, alone with his thoughts, until daylight.

Yoshiko mustered all of her strength to wipe any trace of Yamaga from her memory. She lived her life as before, sleeping all day and staying out half the night. Ordinarily, she didn't get to sleep until morning, when she slept the sleep of the dead, like a stone disappearing into the depths of the dark sea, under a black and moonless sky. Only in the world of her dreams could she find her lost innocence—there among the singing birds and sweet-smelling flowers, without another soul in sight. There was never anyone else there—the world was bright and clear, as though freshly washed. It was a place without family or country; a land without love or hate, or strife. It was a return to the innocence of childhood.

The most difficult time for her was during those moments spent crossing the border between sleep and awakening, when she was tormented by lingering dreams that clutched at her, unwilling to let her go. Her head aching so much it seemed about to split open, Yoshiko suddenly, in a burst of energy, would gather all her strength and will her eyes to open. The sun was setting; a new day was beginning. She would slide out from behind the bed curtains like a wraith, ready to begin another night of excess.

Her schedule was always very full. First, she would have "breakfast," before rounding up her usual gang for another night on the town. They gambled at mah-jongg, poker, and other games of chance that came their way. When they tired of that, they went out drinking, visited nightclubs, or watched operas or concerts. Shanghai was a city that never slept, with nightclubs, dance halls, and tennis courts that stayed open all night.

Yoshiko saw nothing decadent about the life she was leading. Life was short, so why not enjoy it?

Sitting in front of her dressing table and combing her hair
before one such excursion, she evaluated her appearance. Her
short hair looked decent enough—not perfect, but at least it was
smooth and shiny. Her face had a slightly sickly pallor, but that
was easily corrected with a touch of powder, freshly drawn
eyebrows, and a dab of lipstick. She put on one of her favorite
outfits: a black satin scholar's robe, mandarin jacket, and padded
vest, topped off with a little round black satin cap. She looked
for all the world like a casually elegant man-about-town.

That particular evening, she dropped in at the opera house,
trailing an entourage of some dozen hangers-on.

"This way please, Commander Chin," the manager fawned
as he greeted her obsequiously. Bowing and scraping all the way,
he and a waiter led Yoshiko to her seat.

They showed her to a box in the center of the balcony. The
people of Shanghai knew all about her. Some were contemptuous, others despised her, and others still were simply curious, but
none of them dared speak their minds. She was a very powerful
woman, and wherever she went, people rose to their feet and
bowed down, their true feelings well hidden.

Settling in, she put up her feet, and with an air of complete
satisfaction surveyed the theater. The stage was flanked by red-
and-gold lacquered walls, and crimson velvet curtains framed an
actor who, playing a female role, was singing the aria "Raise the
Jade Goblet." The youth looked quite pretty, the result of liberally applied paints and powders, as he coyly refused the goblet
time and time again.

Yoshiko looked on, fanning herself with a black-and-gold
fan, while her other hand rested on the thigh of the handsome

young man beside her. She alternately stroked and squeezed his leg, following the mood of the music. Those around them pretended not to notice. Wasn't life just one great big farce, anyway?

"Bravo!" the audience cried out, cheering the actor whose portrayal of a woman was so convincing.

A boy handed Yoshiko a steaming hand towel sprinkled with rose water, and she wiped off her hands. She recognized him as the flunky she'd sent to check up on Yamaga only a few days before. He was rather good-looking and well built, but his cheap suit gave him a phony air.

Yoshiko took the warm, fragrant towel from him and casually read the note that was concealed beneath it:

"Highbrow" is unreliable.

"Highbrow" was a code name for one of the runners she suspected of leaking information to the other side. There had been three suspects, and to flush out the guilty one, Yoshiko gave each one of them a different set of false information. Then she sat back and waited to see which batch of disinformation was passed to the revolutionaries. It was really quite simple.

Politics was a ruthless game—it was dog-eat-dog. There was no room for dissent. If you allowed dissent, you'd find yourself out in the cold.

The proprietor sent over a tray of tea and snacks. Yoshiko finished wiping off her hands and wadded the note up inside her used towel before handing it back to the boy to take away.

"Please, have some tea," the manager said. "It's top-of-the-line Jade Spring." He smiled ingratiatingly, and she grunted her assent, waiting for him to serve her the tiny porcelain cup of tea. As he passed it to her, he also secretly passed her the stack of bills hidden in his hand. He needed her protection.

With studied nonchalance, Yoshiko picked up her escort's opera glasses and smoothly panned from the corner of the stage to the audience. Her gaze came to rest on one man, and she zoomed in with the binoculars until his magnified face filled her entire field of vision.

He wore a disguise, but Yoshiko recognized him immediately: it was "Highbrow." She pointed the glasses back toward the stage as her boy brought the man some tea. "Highbrow" took a sip and within a second collapsed silently. There was no struggle. The boy and a few adjacent members of the "audience" picked up the body and carried it out.

Yoshiko turned and said to no one in particular, "Let's go. I'm bored."

But she had taken only a few steps when something onstage caught her attention, and she stopped. There was a drumroll, and the audience started cheering wildly. Yoshiko turned to see what all the fuss was about—why, there was a monkey onstage! Soon she realized that it was an actor, but he was so good that he tricked her momentarily. It was a real tour de force. The actor seemed to be half god, half demon—a genius. Capering about lightly in his monkey shirt, monkey pants, and monkey hat, he made monkey faces with his fiery golden eyes. Brandishing a golden staff, he struck fast and sauntered away, then twirled his pole like a big baton, so fast it became a blur, encircling him like a rainbow wheel. He was clearly a master of the martial arts, and his acrobatics were equally impressive. He had the audience eating out of his hand. Yoshiko was seduced as well.

"He's performing *The Monkey King Raises Havoc in Heaven*," the manager said unctuously.

She focused the glasses on the actor, first taking in his body, and then his face. His features were covered in a thick layer of greasepaint, but she felt a nagging sense of recognition.

He was knocking down the assembled hosts of heaven and laughing with glee—just like a happy and excited monkey, clever and quick.

"What's this fellow's name?" Yoshiko asked offhandedly.

"Yun Kai—'Parting Clouds,'" the manager answered promptly. "He's the most famous Monkey King in Shanghai. He brings down the house every time!"

She glanced appraisingly at the stage and then spoke to the manager as though to a pimp:

"Is that so?" she said huskily. "Not bad at all!"

After the performance ended, the crowd poured out of the theater. Outside the main entrance was a marquee with the name Yun Kai emblazoned in large letters, and a poster-sized picture of him to one side. She had only seen that face once, and briefly at that, but it was a face she couldn't forget. He'd made it!

The day she met him on the docks, he was like a young eagle flying from his nest for the first time. Just a few short years had turned that wide-eyed youth into a huge success. The poster frame was edged with a string of bright lights, emphasizing his strong features. She remembered his words to her: "Wait for the parting clouds, and you will see the shining moon."

He looked even more vital and handsome than before.

Ah-fu? Well, not quite. He was Yun Kai now!

A plan already forming in her mind, Yoshiko gave the poster another cursory look before climbing into a small Ford sedan and driving off in a cloud of dust.

15

The sun had not yet set—it was that hour caught between day and night, when the feeble dusk gathers in dim shadows and the colorful lights of the city have not yet winked on. Outside Yoshiko's mansion, a pair of her superficially polite bodyguards were strong-arming a special guest inside.

"I can walk by myself!" he said unhappily.

Somehow he kept his dignity and maintained the impression of the Monkey King striding onstage as they dragged him into the drawing room. He didn't want to be there, but his manager explained to him the importance of cultivating friendships with the rich and powerful, and in the end he really had no choice. The name of his hostess was known to all, for she was a notorious collaborator, and the very thought of her nauseated him—Commander, indeed! He was not a willing guest.

Yoshiko had just taken a sip of very expensive wine when she raised her head and saw that Yun Kai had arrived. She gazed at him steadily, and he stared back, scrutinizing her, and realized with growing shock that he knew her. He was incredulous and stood there numbly, looking as though he'd been dealt a staggering blow.

Was it really her? The owner of the handbag he'd wrested back from that thief, the girl he'd rescued on the quay, that delicate but aloof young lady who came to Shanghai all alone to make a living? She had done more than just make a living, he reflected. She'd made a name for herself, earning wealth, power, and the hatred of millions of Chinese. Yun Kai could not reconcile the girl on the dock with the woman she became. He had trouble regaining his composure. It was like being in the middle of a performance and having a character from an entirely different play suddenly come walking onstage. Everything ground to a halt.

His "hostess" waved her bodyguards off, and they withdrew.

"Sit!" she said, flashing her most charming smile. "It's so wonderful to see you again!" She paused. "Surprised?"

"I'll say! I never imagined that the person who 'invited' me here would turn out to be such a big shot!"

"Really?"

He did not even try to appease her.

"Every red-blooded Chinese has heard of the Kwantung Army's right-hand 'man,' Commander Chin!" He emphasized the word "Commander," speaking it ironically.

She laughed lightly, saying, "Please, call me Yoshiko."

"I don't think I could."

Yoshiko rose and poured him a glass of wine.

"I never forgot you. Who would have thought that in just a few years' time you would become such a great success!"

He felt angry and disappointed—he didn't want to believe that the woman before him was the same woman he'd met on the docks. He wished she were someone else, but the more he wished, the worse he felt. He grappled with his own conflicting feelings, and it was all he could do to restrain himself.

"The same goes for you," he said sarcastically. "I hardly recognized you."

His tone wasn't lost on her.

"So, why did you bring me here?"

Carefully and gracefully, she placed a glass of wine before him and inclined her head.

"Please, have some wine, for old times' sake. If only you could see yourself—you're in quite a state. Or maybe you're simply doing an excellent job playing the self-righteous moralist!"

He took the glass with one hand and set it down on an end table.

"Thanks, anyway!"

He summoned up all his courage and commented:

"I'm afraid your wine would taste of blood."

"Now, that's awfully rude of you, Mr. Yun," she said lightly. She had all the time in the world.

He had no choice but to lift his glass. Throwing his head back, he drained the glass in one gulp and stood up stiffly. He was ready to leave—what was the point of staying?

"I have to go now, Commander Chin, or I'll miss the curtain."

"Does it matter?"

"Yes, it matters!" he snapped. "Being an actor is like being a fireman—you can't just decide not to show up if you don't feel like it; it's not fair to the audience. An actor has a responsibility to make those people sitting in the theater happy."

"Well, you're not making *me* happy," she whined.

She didn't expect him to be such a stubborn and arrogant opponent. Didn't he realize he owed it to her? Until now, she always got the upper hand with men. Was he really immune to her charms? She leaned forward, the surplice of her blouse gapping immodestly, and in her rush to cover herself, she momentarily revealed even more.

Yun Kai looked away.

"That's no use, either!"

Had he really made up his mind not to have anything to do with her? she wondered. Yoshiko drew near to him and lightly squeezed his hand, trying to draw him to her.

"I'm not a Japanese girl. I'm a Chinese girl!" she simpered.

"What are you trying to get at, Commander Chin?"

She was making him uneasy, and his face started to redden. Slinky as a viper, she licked her crimson lips and narrowed her eyes. Then, suddenly, without warning, she burst into wild laughter.

"Ha! Don't you know? Japanese girls can't even compare with Chinese girls, when it comes to the arts of love."

A strange new sensation was churning within him. She was laying a trap for him, and if he fell in, he would never get out alive. As Yoshiko closed in on him, he lost his balance and fell back onto the sofa, but he quickly got back to his feet and pushed her away brusquely.

"Commander Chin—" He hesitated.

"Go on! Say whatever it is you have to say!" She gave him a suggestive sidelong glance. "I like hearing words from the heart."

This was merely part of her seduction, and Yun Kai felt humiliated to see her treasonous face grinning up at him. His anger flared.

"Words from the heart aren't always pretty to hear. I'm not your kept man, Commander Chin. And even if you were mine to do with as I pleased, I don't think I'd be in the mood for you!"

Yun Kai edged toward the door, bowing ceremoniously as he reached the threshold.

"I beg your pardon, miss, but I must take my leave."

He turned and was gone.

Yoshiko flopped down on the sofa and watched him go. She couldn't say he lacked integrity! He chose to have nothing to do with her, and that was that. And the way he looked right through her—did he think he was better than she was? She had wanted to ask him something: "Do you know the secret of my body?" But he didn't give her the chance. Instead, she was made to look like a fool, rebuffed by some two-bit clown. Suddenly, she brightened, as a crafty smile spread across her face. Rising languidly, she strolled over to the telephone, picked up the receiver, and started to dial.

Yun Kai was hurrying back to the theater, his mind already on the performance that lay ahead. He was the handsome Monkey King, wreaker of havoc in heaven! In the play, the Jade Emperor, ruler of all heaven, gave him the impressive title of "Great Sage Who Unifies Heaven" in recognition of his extraordinary abilities. The Jade Emperor was also hoping to harness his great powers to discipline the other members of the heavenly court.

But the Monkey himself was uncontrollable—not only did he steal the Emperor's prized heavenly peaches and the elixir of immortality and demand his freedom, he also took on the powerful armies and generals of heaven—the Eighteen Lohans, the Blue-Faced Monsters, the Gargantuan Spirit General, and the fearsome Female Arhats. One by one, he defeated them with his fancy footwork and wily tricks.

That's me! Yun Kai thought. Puffed up with confidence, he hummed to himself all the way back to theater. When he got there, he headed backstage. But he was in for a very nasty surprise: When he parted the curtain and looked in on that private world where actors are transformed from ordinary people into supernatural beings, he panicked.

The entire backstage area was completely empty. Not a stick of furniture or a thread of a costume remained. It was deserted.

Yun Kai flew into a rage. His scalp was tingling—she was at the bottom of this! He knew it! He gnawed on his lip in agitation. Face livid and neck bulging, he was like a volcano about to blow its top as he stomped out.

For the second time that evening, Yun Kai found himself standing defiantly before Yoshiko Kawashima. He held his arms stiffly at his sides, fists clenched tight. He mustn't let his fury get the better of him.

"So you're back," Yoshiko said, chuckling nonchalantly. "I shall be your sole audience tonight, Master Yun. You'd better perform well and please me!"

All he really had to do to please her was stand there and look handsome—the rest was just icing on the cake. Even the Monkey King finally met his match—in the story it was the Buddha, but in real life it was Yoshiko. There was no escaping her.

Yun Kai's eyes were ablaze.

"Even we actors have our dignity," he said stubbornly. "Do you think you can just snap your fingers and order me around? I don't feel like putting on a show tonight. You might as well just give me back my things and let me be on my way—unless you want to listen to me calling you names all night."

Yoshiko's expression hardened, and she snorted derisively.

"Now, listen here," she said. "I'm the boss around here, and when I say, 'Jump!' you say, 'How high?' Do you understand? You don't have a stage to prance around on unless I give it to you, and the only stage you're going to dance on tonight is right here!"

"Give me back my props, now!" he said intractably.

Smiling icily, Yoshiko motioned to one of her men.

"Bring it all out!"

Moments later, everything was hauled out: instruments, costumes, bits of scenery, costume armor, and costume swords. This mountain of props was followed by quite a crowd of people: string players, drummers, errand boys, and bit players—the entire troupe was there.

"You may leave after your performance," Yoshiko drawled.

"No!" he said fiercely. "I will not be intimidated by you!"

Yoshiko smiled coquettishly.

"If you're going to be like that," she said playfully, "then I'll have to resort to violence."

Completely missing the point, Yun Kai steeled himself, expecting to be beaten. He wasn't afraid of anyone! He would never give in! The miserable and pitiful sound of moaning assailed his ears. It was coming from the other room. His face fell. They were pistol-whipping one of the company's old lute players. Yun Kai appeared unmoved, but he felt sick at heart, and with every dull, thudding blow that fell on the old man's body, he winced involuntarily.

Yoshiko gave a nod, and another member of the company was dragged off. This time the beating was even more furious, but neither begged for mercy—they had their pride.

"Stop it!" Yun Kai shouted suddenly.

He saw Yoshiko's self-satisfied face before him, grinning slyly. She was exultant. She had won! What a fool he was, she reflected. He wouldn't drink the wine of friendship, preferring the poison of animosity. He turned up his nose at the carrot and went for the stick instead. He was stubborn, all right, but he had to realize that he couldn't get away without doing as she asked.

The injured old zither player was tuning his instrument. Nobody else made a sound. It would be a humiliating performance.

Yun Kai brandished the golden staff that was almost a part of him, gripping it tightly with all his strength. Was he really going to perform just for the pleasure of this witch? One by one, his fellow players came by and patted him on the back in sympathy and encouragement, before slipping quietly out.

Yun Kai made his entrance. The drums rolled just as they always did, only this time they conveyed a sense of pent-up anger. In the play, the mighty Monkey King was invincible, but in real life he couldn't even somersault past one tiny woman, who forced him to dance around in her hand to save his comrades.

Yoshiko reclined on the sofa, in an attitude of complete relaxation, following the smooth arcs of his acrobatics with her eyes. Although she seemed to be enjoying herself, she didn't feel entirely satisfied. Whenever he executed a particularly outstanding move, she clapped and called out, "Bravo!"

Yun Kai didn't dare let his resentment boil over. His ego

was bruised, but he still had a spine. Besides, he would never betray his art—he had to give it his all, whatever the circumstances.

He performed only a short act, but this was enough for her, and she took out a thick wad of money and tossed it on a trunk.

"Work for me and I'll pay you double this amount!"

Yun Kai was drenched in sweat, and he mopped himself off with a towel without looking at her.

"We don't want your money!" he hissed between clenched teeth.

"Come, now!" Yoshiko laughed. "Take it, please! You must accept! I wouldn't want people to accuse me, Commander Chin, of abusing my power to get free entertainment. That wouldn't do at all!"

Yoshiko was deeply annoyed, for she *had* used her power and influence. She stole a few minutes of his time and exacted a superficial obedience from him, but in the end, she couldn't have his heart—hers was a hollow victory. After spending all that time and trouble, all she could get out of him was a grudging performance. It was outrageous! She couldn't let him get away with it.

Maybe deep down in her heart, Yoshiko was not so vindictive, but Yun Kai pushed her too far. It was too late.

Yoshiko turned on her heels and left the room. And then she heard it, loud and unmistakable—the sound of breaking glass—as Yun Kai smashed his fist into the mirror in a paroxysm of rage.

There was shattered glass everywhere, and Yun Kai's hand was covered with blood and studded with slivers of the broken mirror. His companions gathered around him, trying to console him with murmured reassurances.

"Never mind the mess. Don't worry."

"Let's put something on your hand to stop the bleeding, Master Yun. Why take it out on yourself?"

"You were forced to perform—it's not your fault."

"We all know you did it for us—"

"What has the world come to? To think that things have gotten so bad that we Chinese are letting a bunch of foreigners and their lapdogs lord it over us!"

Yoshiko overheard some of this, but gradually the voices faded as Yoshiko walked away, out of earshot, head held high.

Yun Kai was still gnashing his teeth.

"I won't forget, Commander Chin. No matter what the price, I will have revenge."

But Yoshiko was gone. Soon after that, she left Shanghai and went to Jehol, in the Northeast.

16

The province of Jehol lay between Mukden Province, in Manchukuo, and Hopei Province, in China. Wealth earned through its principal cash crop of opium made Jehol a desirable possession, and it was only natural that with Manchukuo securely in Japanese hands, Japan's covetous gaze should come to rest on Jehol.

In July of 1932, an officer of the Kwantung Army disappeared while vacationing at a Jehol resort. Seizing on this, the Japanese Army spread a rumor that he had been kidnapped by the Chinese resistance, and, on the pretext of rescuing him, invaded Jehol.

The invasion pressed on—from Yingkou and Shanhai Pass

to Jehol and Chengte. Soon Japan issued a unilateral communiqué declaring that Jehol was now "under the jurisdiction of Manchukuo." The declaration was a political bombshell. Japan was bombarding China on every front.

Countless people lost their lives as Jehol fell to the enemy. Yoshiko was Commander Chin Pi-hui, the heroine of her own Kwantung Army–sponsored fairy tale, lending a hand in the takeover of Jehol with five thousand pacification troops and more than one hundred thousand Japanese yen at her command. Although the takeover was complete, it would be years before things really settled down. The Japanese command had no illusions—there wasn't one Chinese person alive who genuinely wanted friendship and goodwill with the enemy that had invaded his land. "Japanese-Manchurian Friendship" was just a slogan designed to hide the truth from both parties.

As China's provinces fell to Japan one by one, the tide of anti-Japanese sentiment rose ever higher. Some of the most impassioned opponents of Japanese occupation were strong, young Chinese men, and the Japanese struck upon a horribly ingenious way of dealing with them—forcibly injecting them with morphine. Once addicted, they could be written off as harmless. Proud, able-bodied youths were reduced to dull-eyed beggars. There was no one left to fight.

Yoshiko Kawashima didn't care that China's best men were either dead or dying. She was busy playing at soldiers with her Pacification Army, a ragtag band of ruffians. They weren't a regular army at all—they were rounded up with very little attention paid to their qualifications. Her fancy title of commander in chief was just a charade.

Yoshiko toured the still-unpacified province of Jehol several times. Her mission was to coax the insurgents into surrendering, although she made many speeches to the rank and file along the way, indulging her theatrical tendencies. What she liked best about the military life was standing on a podium and declaiming lots of high-sounding phrases into a microphone for the benefit of her troops. The assembled men stood spellbound, in rapt and respectful silence.

"Jehol is in actuality a part of Manchuria," she exclaimed passionately. "It must be reunited with the motherland—Manchukuo. As I speak, our soldiers are out on the front lines. And why are they there? Because they like warfare and are hungry for conquest? No! They are there, ready to fight, and if need be, ready to die, for the common people of Manchukuo and their poor, downtrodden Chinese brethren. These poor people have been abused and reviled by unworthy leaders—we will give them a sense of belonging, we will give them a home, a paradise on earth! Nothing in the world would make your commander happier than to see them happy and prosperous!"

The troops began to applaud, while Yoshiko went on:

"You men who are here today are closest to my heart. I know that the respect is mutual. I have high hopes for you great warriors, I have faith—"

A gunshot cut her short. A sniper from the ranks.

A voice cried out: "Traitor!"

Yoshiko was seriously injured; the bullet had gone through her left shoulder. The searing pain was compounded by her indignation—the shot had been fired by one of her own beloved soldiers. This double blow was more than she could bear.

With great effort, she managed to remain standing and not lose consciousness.

"After him!" she bellowed.

Her underlings plunged into the crowd, seeking out the would-be assassin. Who was he? Every man present was automatically a suspect, and everyone was detained for questioning.

Yoshiko's troops were a motley bunch indeed. They counted among their number small-time hoods, spies, bandits, profiteers, and revolutionaries. Any one of them could have done it.

Yoshiko struggled with all her might, but, unable to hang on any longer, she crumpled to the ground. A bright red bloodstain spread across her uniform.

Paradise on earth, indeed!

How could she deliver something like that when she couldn't even control a paltry five thousand men!

Yoshiko lay in bed, burning with pain and anger. She had endured this agony for thirty hours now, and every time the drugs wore off, the pain seemed even worse than before. The left side of her body was on fire, and her entire body was bathed in sweat. It was like being tied up with barbed wire that tightened with every breath, until it seemed to be driving its thorns into her very bones.

Seeing that the pain was unbearable, her doctor gave her another injection of morphine.

Much later, she opened a weary eye to the hazy outline of a man. It was Shunkichi Uno's aide-de-camp. So, he did care after all, she thought.

She tried to sit up, but her limbs felt like jelly, and she thought she heard her joints scraping together when she moved. Maybe it was just her imagination.

"Commander Chin!" the aide saluted her.

She felt a vague but comforting awareness of a masculine presence.

"Mr. Uno sent me to see how you were feeling."

Yoshiko managed a faint smile as she tried to prop up her sagging spirits.

"It's really not that serious," she said.

The aide took out a velvet-covered box, which opened to reveal a necklace of astounding beauty. Shaped like a phoenix, it was set with nearly a thousand diamonds of every shape and size. It seemed to be spreading its wings to fly. It was an exquisite piece, and priceless.

"Please accept this small token of Mr. Uno's friendship, Commander Chin."

Pleasure and excitement filled Yoshiko's face as she stroked the necklace. There was a reward for her suffering, after all.

The aide was still speaking, blandly conveying his superior's messages.

"Mr. Uno says he hopes that you will get some rest so that you can make a full recovery from your injuries. You mustn't worry about your work—it can be handed over to others. The most important thing is for you to rest. Please do not worry. Your duties are in good hands, and you may rest assured everything will be fine without you."

He spoke very politely, as if he were only concerned for her welfare, but he was *too* polite. As Yoshiko listened, her expression gradually changed, ever so subtly. The smile never left her face, for she was good at hiding her feelings, but she went pale. The implications of Uno's message were all too clear. This was the prelude to being shut out of power entirely. Shunkichi Uno thought she was a burden, did he? He'd decided she had outlived her usefulness, had he? After she helped them found Manchukuo, by spreading propaganda, giving out bribes, putting the squeeze on politicians, spying, and bringing the populace to heel, was this how they showed their gratitude? Were they unwilling to forgive her even one tiny slip? It would have been much more convenient for them if that bullet had killed her. But she lived.

She was an aristocrat, a princess, a member of the Ching

imperial family, who fought bravely for their common cause. The founding of Manchukuo was the fruit of her labors; but now that Manchukuo was secure, was she to be forgotten? Were her dreams of grandeur to be stripped from her?

She couldn't believe life was so cruel; but even if it was, she refused to be daunted. She would fight until the bitter end. Nobody could just use her up and spit her out. She wouldn't permit it!

Her smiling face still brimmed with excitement.

"Please tell Daddy 'thank you' for me!"

Uno's aide took his leave.

Yoshiko regarded the ice-cold phoenix. It was just a bunch of dirt and rocks, she reflected. Things were only as valuable as people thought they were, diamonds included. She was still worth something, she thought defiantly.

The shadows of night slowly gathered, encroaching bit by bit on the snowy whiteness of Yoshiko's hospital room. There was something lonely and empty, and a bit melancholy, about all that white; but as the shadows invaded it, Yoshiko burst into uncontrollable tears. It wasn't fair! It was all that sniper's fault! She despised him!

Life was cruel, but she would beat it at its own game!

When the tree falls, the monkeys scatter—so the old saying goes. And if you cut off the head, the rest of the body dies with it. Yoshiko wanted to get to the bottom of the plot against her—she wanted the ringleader.

Her wound still wasn't healed, and she needed daily injections of morphine for the pain, but her thirst for revenge drove her on. She sat in the dank underground prison, eyes glowering and jaw clenched, personally interrogating each day's fresh batch of suspects. Most of them served under her as pacification troops, and one by one they were rounded up and brought in. Anguished shrieks and moans reached Yoshiko's ears from time to time, like the cries of the damned suffering the torments of hell. The prisoners were all guilty until proven innocent, but the ones whom the jailers hated the most, the ones who would rather die than submit, were members of the anti-Japanese resistance. Their captors devised many different ways of dealing with their stubbornness.

They used awls and needles to turn prisoners into men of blood, and if their victim happened to glare back at them or curse them, they poked out the offending eyes so that the blood gushing from those empty sockets covered the victim's entire face. This only made the torturers laugh. Sometimes they took red-hot irons, which, when dipped into buckets of water, made such loud hissing and billowing clouds of steam that the victims were frozen with terror. Then the interrogators laid these irons on their victim's chests; the cooked flesh gave off a foul odor. They hung the more difficult prisoners from the walls by their thumbs and left them there to die.

Or the torturers might make a strong solution of chilies mixed with water and force it into a prisoner's mouth and nose. The peppers were so hot that the man's face grew red and swollen, and blood oozed out of his ears and mouth. They liked to pour water down a man's throat until the skin of his belly was as tight as a drum, but they didn't stop there. They just kept on pumping it in until he swelled up like a big balloon; and when they could force no more water in, the interrogators stepped onto the victim's belly, killing him instantly as water gushed from every orifice.

Even the toughest prisoner couldn't hold up when he lay

on his back with his body roped tightly to one wooden stool and his feet tied to another stool, while they placed a brick on his knees every time he refused to answer a question. They loaded on the bricks until the man's joints bowed backward under the weight, making a gut-wrenching crack.

They also lashed their captives with bullwhips, hung them from their heels, put them on the rack, drew their blood, injected them with air, stuck thin strips of bamboo under their fingernails, shone blinding lights into their eyes, or slowly hacked them to bits, one piece at a time, as they lay helpless and unable to move. This was the price of resistance.

The Kwantung Army had been carrying out the day's round of tortures for some time when Yoshiko arrived at the prison, eager to confront her would-be assassin and exact her revenge.

He was a young man, in his twenties, with strong eyebrows, large eyes, and thick lips that gave him a somewhat idiotic expression. Closer inspection revealed that the torturer's art had thickened his lips. He was covered with blood, but when he still refused to speak, a pair of wardens held him down and pried open his mouth while a third took a file and began to grind down his teeth. Each stroke sent a shock through his skull, and his whole body shuddered.

The very sight of him sent Yoshiko into a rage, and she grabbed him roughly with one hand. The motion was too hard and fast for her unhealed wound, and searing pain made her break into a cold sweat.

"Who put you up to it?" she demanded harshly.

He didn't respond and tried to turn his head away, but she wasn't going to let him off.

"Speak! How many are there in your organization?"

The man's teeth dangled loose in his gums, swimming in a sea of blood. He refused to look at her, and she shook him furiously.

"I'm in control here—so don't think that I won't find out who they are!" she shrieked hysterically. "Every one of my pacification troops will be interrogated—all five thousand of them, one man at a time—until I find the others. If you refuse to talk, the blood of many innocent men will be on your hands. Tomorrow—"

She was cut short by a huge, bloody gob of spit. The rotten, slimy mixture of blood, saliva, and chunks of teeth struck her squarely in the face. His features were no longer recognizable, but he was still human, and he knew that he did not have long to live, so he bravely plunged on, cursing her:

"I'd rather die than tell you anything! The people of China spit on you! Traitor! Whore!" He could barely speak, but she heard every word loud and clear as he unleashed a torrent of abuse. "You'll die like a dog!"

Shaking with fury, the veins on her temples throbbing with each rasping breath she took, Yoshiko snatched up a red-hot poker and, without a moment's hesitation, thrust it straight into the man's mouth and ground it from side to side in a frenzy. He died instantly.

The force of Yoshiko's exertions broke open her own wound, which started to ooze blood. Like a wounded animal, she was enraged by pain. This man had hurt her, and if she let him get away with it, she would be nothing but the hollow shell of a woman, robbed of power and dignity.

"I owe you one, you bastard!" she screeched as she pulled out her pistol. She fired wildly all around her, and the bullets whizzed into the prison, popping and spitting like a raging flame. Prisoners fell left and right, struck down by this wanton barrage.

Her gun was empty, but she was still filled with rage.

She hadn't slept well in nearly a month. Nerves on edge, she was constantly on guard against other conspiracies. Lying awake at night, she stared up at the ceiling. The tiniest sound made her sit bolt upright in bed and fire her gun at the wall. There were bullet holes everywhere.

She finally left Jehol and went back to Japan to recuperate, although it was just as good as being under house arrest.

Meanwhile, the Japanese Army was tightening its stranglehold on China. Setting out from its base in Manchuria, it marched across North China, occupying one place at a time, establishing racial-quarantine areas where the conquered people could be watched and controlled. Resistance against Japan was a contagion—its spread had to be stopped.

There were militiamen, military police, spies, and traitors everywhere, and they arrested and murdered people as they pleased. During this reign of terror, famous people were kidnapped, and ordinary folk simply kept quiet. The Nationalist government did not put up a fight, and many good men were dragged off to be tortured to death as a result. Women in the city and countryside were raped, often gang-raped. Later, they would be found, with their clothing torn, their breasts cut off, their bellies sliced open, and their vaginas stuffed with wood, bamboo poles, or wadded-up newspaper.

Young patriots, many of them students, marched in the pouring rain, carrying their protest to the streets and alleys of China.

"Down with Japanese militarism!"

"Invaders go home!"

"Down with Manchukuo! Down with Japan!"

"Boycott Japanese goods!"

"Down with stinking spies and traitors!"

"Oppose the policy of Nonresistance!"

"Chinese people unite!"

"Give us back our countrymen! Give us back our country!"

"Debts of blood must be repaid in blood!"

The marchers were like a mighty sea, surging and cresting. They were the indomitable soul of the Chinese nation. No rain, no matter how torrential, could quench the fires that burned in these people's hearts.

United in spirit, they endured the shame of occupation and oppression. Many hot-blooded idealists lost their jobs and left their homes and families to join the resistance. Until they had a country, they couldn't really say they had homes. And what was one life, compared to the fate of an entire nation? They were prepared to lay down their lives at a moment's notice.

In the middle of the throng of demonstrators, proudly scrubbed clean of his greasepaint, was Yun Kai. Onstage, he was the center of attention, commanding all that he surveyed; but swept up in this mighty current, he was only one of many staunch patriots. He had no regrets.

One night, in a dark corner of the opera company's tent, a dozen or so shadowy figures huddled together in the darkness. Somebody had angrily drawn a big X across an official portrait of Yoshiko Kawashima and Shunkichi Uno.

A map lay to one side. It was a floor plan of a restaurant called Tung-hsing Lou.

17

After three years in Japan, Yoshiko had returned to China, this time making Tientsin her base of operations. Not far from Peking, Tientsin was an important military and diplomatic center. It was also a very prosperous city, and in the Japanese concession, on Matsushima Road, there stood a splendid and imposing building that housed an elegant Chinese restaurant: Tung-hsing Lou.

Shunkichi Uno provided this place for Yoshiko. But it was not just a place for her—it also served as a gathering place for the various soldiers, irregulars, and bullyboys of the all but defunct Pacification Army. That pseudo-army was as good as disbanded, but Yoshiko clung stubbornly to the now empty title of "commander in chief"—it was just about all she had left. Her subordinates couldn't go home because anti-Japanese feeling was at a fever pitch, and they sought refuge and a few bowls of rice at her place. They had nowhere else to go.

Today, a festive atmosphere filled the restaurant—in sharp contrast to the rest of China, where the streets ran with blood. Half of the country was already in enemy hands, and Japan was poised to deliver the fatal blow.

Meanwhile, Pu-yi temporarily left behind the illusory glory of his Manchukuo court and paid a visit to Japan, sailing from Dairen on a Japanese ship. In Tokyo, he paid his respects to the emperor Hirohito, and together they reviewed the troops and worshiped at the Meiji Shrine. Puffed up with false pride, the "emperor" Pu-yi issued a sycophantic decree called the "Returning Emperor's Edict to His Obedient People" as soon as he returned to Hsinching. Everyone in Manchukuo—old and young, rich and poor—was summoned to meetings held in public places of all kinds: schools, military barracks, and government offices. There, everyone had to memorize the edict as a demonstration of goodwill and respect for Japan.

All over the Northeast, Pu-yi installed Shinto shrines in which he placed relics like the ones he brought back from Japan—a sword, a brass mirror, and a jade hook. Services were held at the appropriate times, and he further decreed that whenever anyone passed by the front of such a temple, he must bow no fewer than ninety times.

The edict was the emperor's in name only—the real author of this decree was a Kwantung Army staff officer, Pu-yi's puppeteer, Yasunori Yoshioka, officially a royal adviser.

Yoshioka was speaking slowly to Pu-yi, a false smile pasted on his face.

"Japan is like Your Majesty's father, you see? And the Kwantung Army is Japan's representative here. So you see, the commander of the Kwantung Army is also Your Majesty's father, isn't he?"

Japanese troops poured across Manchukuo and North China, heading straight toward their goals: Peking, Shanghai, and Nanking. The status of the puppet emperor of Manchukuo slipped ever lower, until he found himself a mere "child" in the political arena. Even his own personal weapons were confiscated.

Pu-yi's younger brother, Pu-chieh, submitted to military orders and married Hiro Saga, the daughter of Duke Masaru Saga, in Tokyo, and the Japanese issued a decree based on the laws of imperial succession:

Should the emperor die, he would be succeeded by his son. If he should die without sons, then he should be succeeded by his grandson. Should there be no living sons or grandsons, then his younger brother should succeed him. However, if his younger brother does not survive him, then his younger brother's son would succeed.

The Kwantung Army wanted an emperor with Japanese blood, but in the event that Pu-yi had a son, he would be sent to Japan to be raised by militarists. These facts remained hidden from Pu-yi behind the smiling faces of his Japanese advisers.

Tung-hsing Lou was an impressive restaurant indeed, and like a duplicitously smiling face, it welcomed the puppet commander Chin Pi-hui. Nobody could accuse the Kwantung Army of treating her badly.

The magnificent restaurant was festooned with flowers: garlands, wreaths, and baskets brimming with flowers. A huge red banner over the front door read CLOSED FOR OWNER'S BIRTHDAY

BANQUET. In addition to the main dining room, there were private rooms upstairs and open-air gazebos in the garden. Today, the main dining room was set up for a big birthday party.

Yoshiko appeared to put the finishing touches on the preparations. She still often liked to dress in men's clothing. Today, she wore a long gray robe of silk and linen embroidered with clouds and with the character for "Long Life" woven in. Over this, she wore a tunic. Coupled with these, the ivory folding fan she held in one hand made her a portrait in gray and white, which was set off by the intense black of her eyes and brows and the crimson of her lipstick. Her makeup came across as overly theatrical and somewhat tawdry; but even with her overdone makeup, she still looked unfinished. Something was missing—something indefinable.

Before any of the guests arrived, an intriguing package was delivered, and Yoshiko's secretary Chizuko signed for it. After lifting the contents out of their box, she pushed aside the cloth draped over it, revealing a brightly polished silver plaque inscribed with the words HAPPY BIRTHDAY YOSHIKO KAWASHIMA, FROM COMMANDER SHUNKICHI UNO, NORTH CHINA EXPEDITIONARY FORCE.

"Miss Yoshiko," Chizuko reported, "the silver plaque has arrived."

"Is it engraved as I ordered?"

"Yes, miss. The inscription says that it is a gift from Mr. Uno."

"Good. Please display it in the center of the main hall so that everyone can see it!"

Chizuko nodded discreetly.

"When Mr. Uno shows up," Yoshiko reminded her, "let me know right away!"

"Yes, Miss Yoshiko."

Yoshiko admired this "birthday present" that she herself had commissioned on the sly, feeling rather pleased with herself. This silver plaque flaunted her continued close relationship with a very important person. It was a silent symbol of power and influence, proof that she, Yoshiko Kawashima, Commander Chin Pi-hui, was still valuable in Shunkichi Uno's eyes. And who had time to delve into the secret of the silver plaque?

Yoshiko inspected the plaque closely, cocked her head, backed up a bit to give it another appraisal, and moved it a few inches. It had to look just right. She narrowed her eyes, feeling the thrill of a child who is getting away with something, but it hurt her at the same time. Who could tell what she really felt? Who could tell who she really was? She looked like a young man of twenty, but in fact she was already past thirty. And while she was supposed to be celebrating her birthday today, she didn't really want to count the years. How many good years did she have left? Were the best years of her life already past? Would those days of patriotic activism ever return? She had to face it, she was getting older by the minute. Fortunately, her captivating beauty had not yet deserted her, although she could feel it starting to slip away.

People were calling out to her:

"Commander Chin!"

"Miss Yoshiko!"

"Eastern Jewel!"

"Princess Hsien-tzu!"

"Fourteenth Princess!"

One by one, her guests filed in, different guests calling her by different names. The head of the North China Governing Committee's Office of Information, the minister of internal affairs of Manchukuo, and a minister from the Japanese Ministry of Industry and Trade were there. There were also advisers from the Japanese and Manchurian embassies, journalists, Japanese actors and actresses, stars of the Chinese stage, bank managers, theater managers, and officers from the Japanese Imperial Army. Every man was dressed to the nines, and every woman was poised and elegant. Their gifts were the best that money could buy—or sometimes just a large sum of money. On the surface, at least, everyone paid homage to Yoshiko.

Just as she was about to go and greet another guest, Old Wang, one of her translation officers, brought a sad-eyed, middle-aged man over to her.

"Commander Chin," Old Wang said humbly. "This is Mr. Chu. He would be extremely grateful if you would speak with him for a moment."

"Chu, did you say?" She furrowed her brow. "It's that business about the man with the silk shop, isn't it? Well, I'm afraid I don't have time right now. Some other time—"

"Please, Commander Chin," Mr. Chu cut in. "Please help us. My brother is in prison, probably being tortured at this very moment. He's not a young man anymore. He won't be able to last long."

"Has he confessed to anything?" Yoshiko asked Old Wang.

"They tried to beat a confession out of him, but he didn't tell them anything useful."

Although Mr. Chu was a proud man, he couldn't hold back his tears.

"It's all a mistake, Commander. The charges are false! Please, say a few words on his behalf!"

"If this brother of yours is an anti-Japanese guerrilla, then there's really nothing I can do," she said impatiently.

"Please, miss, don't make fun of us. We are an old Peking

family, and we've never concerned ourselves with anything but selling silk. My brother is over fifty years old—he doesn't have the muscle to play soldier! We are just ordinary citizens."

Ever since Mr. Chu's brother's arrest, the family had been scurrying around from place to place, trying to find a way to get him released. At last they got access to Yoshiko through Old Wang. They were so desperate, they would grasp at anything, like shipwrecked passengers clutching at splinters to keep from drowning. Commander Chin was their salvation, they thought, a giant life raft—but her reputation and power were greatly inflated. Mr. Chu had to "go through the back door," as the Chinese say—use his connections—to get close to Yoshiko, and this process entailed handing out all kinds of valuable gifts and greasing many palms along the way. Otherwise, he wouldn't even have got his foot in the door; although perhaps "foot in the door" was the wrong expression—it was more like putting his foot into a trap.

"Today is my birthday!" Yoshiko said irritably. "Why did you have to pick a day like this to come pestering me?"

"Please," Mr. Chu pleaded tearfully. "Please, just have a few words with your friends in the Imperial Army. We can come up with twenty thousand yuan. Please help us, Commander Chin!"

"That amount may not be enough to cover it—still, I'll see what I can do. But I can't make any promises."

"But, Commander, twenty thousand is a lot of money—"

Old Wang took him aside and gave him the word: In all likelihood, Chu would have to come up with sixty thousand yuan before the matter was concluded. It was an astronomical bribe, but it was also a matter of life and death. It broke Mr. Chu's heart to be haggling over money while his brother's life hung in the balance.

Yoshiko left them to work it out and headed for the main

dining room. She knew that they would ultimately agree upon a price—say, 30,000 to 40,000. Then she could use her influence to put some pressure on the military police. All it took was one phone call to an easily intimidated subordinate officer—there was no need to disturb the higher-ups—and the prisoner would be released. Wherever there were Chinese, there was always a "back door," she reflected.

Flashbulbs were popping left and right. Yoshiko moved through the crowd of well-wishers like a butterfly fluttering from one flowering bush to another, circulating among her distinguished guests, stopping just long enough to pose for photos with them before she moved on.

Everyone was superficially polite, but many people there scoffed at her behind her back.

An officer and an ambassador were talking:

"They call her Commander, but it's all a charade as far as I'm concerned!"

"How could a woman do anything important in the first place?"

"Well, she has managed to gather some amazingly detailed and accurate information. Did you know that Chiang Kai-shek's Nationalist government is willing to agree to a cease-fire with Japan in exchange for staying in power? Those Nationalists are more worried about the Communists right now than they are about the Japanese!"

"They're afraid the Communists will take advantage of their role in the resistance to expand their power base."

"While the Chinese are busy fighting among themselves, the Imperial Army can just walk right in!"

"Wasn't that little honey pot the source of all that news?"

"Damn right, she was! We men are all alike!" He laughed. "Every man is a lecher at heart!"

"And what about you? Have you been with her?"

"Shh—"

Just then Yoshiko walked up to them.

"Mr. Sasaki," she chided the officer. "What are you doing at my birthday party with that dreadful little rag hanging out of your pocket? Is it some kind of good-luck charm?"

His face grew solemn.

"Many different women toiled long and hard to sew this cloth. It is the custom in Japan to give these to soldiers when they go off to war, with the wish that they may fight well and return victorious. I never put on my uniform without tucking this into my pocket. Don't you know about this custom, Miss Yoshiko?"

"I'm a soldier, too! Where is my little hanky?" She smiled coquettishly and added, "We women are always pinning our hopes on men. I don't know if we're extremely clever or extremely stupid!"

Yoshiko kept up this stream of banter, but her lively eyes swept over the room all the while, constantly searching: The face she sought was not there. Wouldn't Shunkichi Uno, the man she still called "Daddy" in a pathetic attempt to keep in his good graces, toss her even this tiny crumb?

The banquet was beginning, with a first course of assorted appetizers already laid out on the round tables that filled the room. Waiters poured three-star brandy into crystal wineglasses, and Yoshiko called out from her seat at the head table:

"Please, everybody, help yourselves—but save some room for the other courses! We're going to treat you to a marvelous feast tonight. You know, people say that the best Tientsin dish is meat dumplings from Kou-pu-li, but I can't say I've ever tried them. In fact, China is the home of much fine cuisine, like Mongolian hot pot. . . ."

She glanced furtively at her watch. When she looked up, she saw Uno's assistant coming her way.

"Miss Yoshiko," he said formally. "Mr. Uno had some business to attend to, and he sends his regrets. I am here in his stead to convey to you his best wishes on your birthday."

Not him again! she thought to herself. Once more Uno was sending a flunky in his place. Didn't she count for anything anymore? He wouldn't even show up this one day of the year!

As the waiters rushed to set a place for Uno's deputy, a flash of displeasure crossed Yoshiko's face, but she forced herself to smile.

"Oh well, I guess Daddy is very busy these days. I just hope he won't disappoint me next year!"

The main courses were brought out, carried by wave after wave of uniformed servants. There were delicacies of every kind—game, poultry, seafood, all of it the best. The banquet tables were buried under dishes—not an inch of tabletop peeked through anywhere—and Yoshiko enjoyed a brief reprieve from her embarrassment as the partygoers turned their full attention to the delicacies set before them. The hall was crowded with Yoshiko's guests, but none of them were her real friends. Toadies and sycophants surrounded her on all sides. Politics was a treacherous business.

She lived in a fantasy world, for she met every crisis with self-deception—it was the only way to survive. The truth would destroy her, but she was growing tired of lying to herself. Ten long years of living like this—they'd passed in the blink of an eye. She couldn't give up now! She had to get back into the ring and defend her title. But she was exhausted.

The nagging pain of Yoshiko's old wound penetrated the gaiety of the occasion, and an odd grin crept slowly across her face as she nonchalantly reached across to a drawer in the side-board behind her and took out a needle and a vial of white powder. With one eye on her guests, she deftly lifted the hem of her long white tunic, rolled up a pants leg, and injected the needle into her calf, all without a trace of embarrassment.

Silence fell on the hall—her guests stared, speechless. She closed her eyes and let out a long, dreamy sigh. When she opened her eyes, they were sparkling again, and she put the needle away as everyone looked on. Turning back toward her assembled guests, she addressed them with a slight tilt of her head:

"Sometimes my old wound bothers me, and I need an injection. Afterward, I can't drink water—but spirits are just fine. Cheers! Bottoms up, everyone!"

Just as she was raising her brandy glass high to make the toast, there was sudden burst of gunfire. Her glass shattered into a thousand pieces, and Yoshiko's white cuff was sprayed with the amber-colored liquor.

The banquet was under attack by members of the resistance who infiltrated the party disguised as servants and guests. Bullets were flying everywhere, and acrid smoke filled the room.

The crisis sobered Yoshiko like ice water flung in her face, and without a moment's hesitation she rolled underneath the table. The guerrillas first took aim at Uno's deputy, one of the Japanese officers on their hit list; but their principal targets were Shunkichi Uno and Yoshiko Kawashima. What nobody there knew was that Uno had found out about the plot and decided to stay home.

The attackers rushing forward in search of Yoshiko met with her bullets, instead. She was still a good shot, even when taking aim from the limited vantage point underneath a table. She was furious—in an instant, her splendid birthday party had been transformed into a battlefield. Blood-spattered plates and bowls were scattered everywhere, and men and women who only minutes before had been drinking and laughing lay dead or wounded.

Yoshiko managed to hit two of the interlopers, one of whom she caught in the thigh. As he stumbled and fell, his hat slipped to reveal his face—a face she knew well. Yun Kai!

After that night at her mansion in Shanghai, Yun Kai had dropped out of sight. He quit singing opera—it was somehow tainted. He threw away a brilliant career, all because of his stubbornness. Because of Yun Kai's attitude, Yoshiko came to reserve a special hatred for theater people, and many prominent actors suffered as a consequence. Stars like Ma Lien-liang, Cheng Yen-chiu, Hsin Yen-chiu, and Pai Yu-shuang were blackmailed and humiliated. Still, Yoshiko continued to invite anyone who played the Monkey King to her parties, but Yun Kai was never among them. A star is always in command onstage, but in real life it was Yoshiko whose power shone brightest. It never crossed her mind that she, too, might end up as just a character in somebody else's play. The man who had left an indelible mark on her, whom she desired most of all but could not attain, had banded together with a bunch of hoods to kill her!

When she realized it was Yun Kai, she was torn, not knowing whether she should simply finish him off with one more shot. Her anger told her to pull the trigger, but something, some inner weakness, made her hesitate, and in the end she couldn't do it. Looking at this brave and committed young man, she was filled with a kind of wonder. He was still so young, so inexperienced—he'd hardly had a chance to live yet, but he was willing to die for his beliefs. After basking in the limelight for a few brief seasons, he cast it all away to become an outlaw fighter.

Yoshiko and the military police quickly restored order. Although seriously wounded, Uno's deputy took charge of a team and went outside to stand guard. Uno had chosen his man well, but he had no intention of letting Yoshiko find out about his treachery.

Some of the resistance men who had attacked died. The survivors, some twenty in all, were arrested. Yoshiko stood among the wreckage, watching as Yun Kai was taken away. His wounded leg was bleeding profusely, and as he was unable to walk, the police had to half carry him away, leaving a trail of blood so wide it seemed to have been painted by a giant brush.

Long after everyone else was gone, Yoshiko was still staring at the glistening red path that led straight out the grand entryway of the Tung-hsing Lou restaurant. Even if he was the ringleader . . . she thought to herself. Seized by a sudden impulse, she jumped to her feet and rushed out.

It was late at night when Yoshiko appeared outside the Tientsin Military Headquarters Prison. The officer on duty greeted her respectfully—she still carried a bit of clout, after all. The title of Commander was still hers, and she knew how to use it.

It wasn't long before a pair of wardens dragged in Yun Kai, half-dazed from hours of torture. She motioned the wardens, and they withdrew, but the duty officer looked uncomfortable and hesitated.

"Miss Yoshiko—" he ventured.

"When something like this happens on my birthday, at my birthday banquet," she cut him off darkly, "I take it personally. The responsibility quite clearly falls to me to see that the matter is taken care of satisfactorily. I will hand this matter over to Mr. Shunkichi Uno myself."

She left with a flourish, her "prisoner" in tow.

18

Yun Kai didn't know where he was. With great effort, he managed to open his eyes just a crack, and the darkness that engulfed him gradually cleared. He was shivering as he regained consciousness, for he had lost a great deal of blood. Even the slightest movement was excruciatingly painful, and every vein in his body felt as though it were filled with lead. His legs felt especially heavy, and he moaned faintly as he tried to move them.

He looked around at the unfamiliar surroundings. Where was he? His head was cradled on a soft pillow on a high bed, in a sumptuously feminine boudoir. A pleasantly sweet perfume hung in the air, and Japanese woodblock prints of geishas graced the walls, smiling down on him and the three other people in the room.

The mood became even more voluptuous as a blind musician in one corner began to play an indolent, sensual tune on the samisen. Alone in his dark world, the musician was oblivious to those outside, unaware of what kind of people they were. He was soon lost in the melody that flowed from his fingers.

Yoshiko sat beside the bed in a pearl-colored nightdress. Just a shade off white, it was also the color of an oyster, that mysterious animal that seeks to transform, by its smooth and pale example, the grains of sand that work their way into its flesh. Through constant struggle, the oyster always triumphs, coating the sharp and irregular grains with fluids from its own body until they become perfectly round and luminous, and almost white.

The doctor gathered up his instruments and left, but Yoshiko remained sitting by the bed, a glass of wine in her hand, gazing at Yun Kai. After a long while, she took a sip of wine, then went back to waiting patiently at his side. He was her witness, she thought to herself. His very presence here was proof of her goodness. She had gone to great lengths to bring him here.

An indescribable sense of peace flowed from the samisen, as Yoshiko quietly savored Yun Kai's moaning. The anesthetic was wearing off, and his groans became louder. Taking out her needle, Yoshiko readied the clear morphine solution and walked over to the bed, where she ever so gently lifted up his thigh. It was firm and well formed—he had the body of a fighter. Capable of striking hard and fast, at this moment Yun Kai was as limp as a sleeping baby. Yoshiko lightly rolled up his tunic and pants leg and wiped away the bloodstain. With practiced fingers, she pressed and probed until she found his vein, a vital dark blue serpent. Placing the tip of the needle against his skin, she released the morphine into his blood very, very slowly. He flinched weakly but gradually relaxed as a warm wave of pure happiness washed over his body, engulfing him like a sweet dream from which he never wanted to awaken. When the syringe was empty, Yoshiko tenderly massaged the almost invisible little hole where the needle had pierced his flesh. The pain was gone now, and he felt at peace.

He sighed lightly, a faint smile playing at his lips. He was as helpless as a baby and, in this semiconscious state, lacked the will to deceive himself—he saw that the woman sitting before him was very pretty. Freed from worry and inhibition, feeling neither fear nor animosity, he forgot who he was. He had a sensation that was like the gentle caress of a spring breeze, or the first tentative thaw after a heavy snow. Was it just the drug that made him feel this way? Or was it something more? Entranced by the spell of her beauty, he was transported back to their first meeting.

He reached out, and she grasped his hand, placing it on her left breast. Only a thin layer of silk separated his hand from that carefully guarded treasure.

She felt as though the world had been completely cleansed—purified for this new beginning, and a maternal feeling welled up in her as Yun Kai fell into a deep sleep. She felt like a mother welcoming back an errant child, her own flesh and blood. She had only hated him because he had hated her. The hard lines of her face softened—she might be capable of murdering anyone in the world, but she could never harm him. Even if she spent the rest of her life in solitude, she would always have this night, she reflected as she gazed down at him and gently stroked his handsome face.

"Ah-fu," she whispered softly.

The old samisen master was singing in his quavering voice, telling an ancient Japanese tale to the strains of the samisen:

Throughout recorded time,
All living things have been at war.
Spring flowers turn to dust,
As white bones turn to ash.
But the river flows ever on, ever on,
Red leaves dance wildly in the wind. . . .

The soothing melody carried her away, but she was jolted out of her reverie by the harsh bell of the telephone. Feeling somewhat disoriented at first, she heard the person on the other end of the line speaking to her in a foreign language—Japanese. It was one of Uno's flunkies. She was back in the real world.

The Lucky Crane was the most expensive restaurant in Tientsin. Located in the Japanese concession, it was also the only place in town that served fugu, puffer fish. A pair of large, round puffer-fish-shaped lanterns hanging in front of the shop announced this fact. Fugu was a Japanese delicacy that had to be prepared with great care by a trained master—an improperly cleaned fish could be lethal. The Lucky Crane's proprietor had twenty-five years' experience in preparing fugu and had come to China to open a business that catered to a Japanese clientele. It was currently the height of the fugu season, and some especially large and plump fish had just come in. Tonight, the entire restaurant was reserved for a private party. The host: Shunkichi Uno. Yoshiko was on the guest list.

This rather astounded her. Why had he bothered to get in touch with her? she wondered. What business did he want with her? Was it about Yun Kai? She would have to be very careful.

One of the courses was puffer-fish fins, roasted over coals until they were half-cooked and then poached in warm sake. Eaten lukewarm, they had an unusual and slightly smoky flavor. It was definitely an acquired taste.

Yoshiko raised her glass.

"Here's to you, Daddy!"

Uno pinched her cheek. "You've gotten a bit thin."

"If you saw me more often," she said testily, "little changes in my appearance wouldn't seem so sudden."

He picked up a thin morsel of fish with his chopsticks and popped it into his mouth, fixing her with a steady gaze as he chewed.

"Rumor has it that you took a resistance man home with you," he said offhandedly.

"He was involved in that riot at Tung-hsing Lou," she answered quickly. "I had to interrogate him personally, of course."

She poured him a cup of sake and then poured one for herself.

"Where are you holding him?"

Uno knew perfectly well where Yun Kai was, but his smooth voice betrayed nothing.

"When did you start concerning yourself with my methods of interrogation?" Yoshiko laughed.

"I trust you implicitly, of course," he said.

Afraid of giving herself away, Yoshiko moved to pour more wine.

"Have another cup," she offered him.

"I don't think I'll have any more. I need to keep a clear head. Too much drink affects my judgment. You shouldn't drink too much either, you know."

"Don't worry about me!" she snapped. "I know the difference between what's business and what's personal!"

A moment later, she said sheepishly, "I haven't had a drink with you in so long—am I still the samurai's sword?"

Uno laughed heartily, but he didn't touch his drink.

"If you could only see yourself!"

The proprietor himself was serving them, and he now brought out a porcelain plate with a fine multicolored glaze. A circle of thinly sliced fugu was arranged on the plate in the shape of a chrysanthemum in full bloom. Yoshiko took a bite, and the flavor was very delicate. She changed the subject.

"It's nice and sweet. It tastes very fresh!"

"We have a saying in Japan," Uno said casually. "People who eat fugu are idiots; and people who don't eat fugu are idiots, too."

She knew he was trying to get at her, but how much did he really know?

He went on.

"Fugu has a very fast-acting venom, which is often lethal. People who eat fugu are stupid, because they risk death with every bite. On the other hand, people who are afraid to try it are equally stupid, because they're missing out on one of life's choicest delicacies. Do you like fugu, Yoshiko?"

"Yes, I do. Very much," she replied calmly. "This isn't the first time I've eaten it, you know. If you eat a lot of fugu, you can build up a resistance to the venom and become immune to a host of other poisons, besides. So the more you eat, the longer you'll live!"

Uno let out a burst of amused laughter that stopped just as abruptly as it started. He searched her face, hoping to find some crack in her armor, but his quicksilver changes of mood put

Yoshiko on her guard. She uneasily tossed some vegetables and bean curd into the clear, boiling broth of the hot pot they were sharing, her movements a bit too hurried. Everything was dancing and churning in the bubbling soup. The flame was very hot.

"It's ready."

She took out a few slices of cooked fish and carefully set them on his plate.

"Some people say that women are like cats—both are attracted to the smell of fish," he said. "The Chinese say that once a cat bites down on a fish, it's all but impossible to take it away."

"You know a lot about the Chinese, don't you, Daddy?"

She thought she detected a note of jealousy in his voice. Then again, perhaps it wasn't jealousy at all, but rather her own wishful thinking. Sometimes she wished she were still his personal property, but she understood him too well. It was only his male desire to control that caused that possessive note to creep into his voice. Even if he didn't think very much of her anymore, news of her other lovers pricked him—like a fish bone stuck in his throat, not coming up or going down. So tiny, yet so irritating—and dangerous, too. If it went the wrong way, you could be paralyzed.

"Chinese folk sayings are fascinating. But that's the problem with the Chinese—even when they die, their mouths just keep on talking, heaping insults on each other. What a third-rate nation! You probably hate China, too, don't you, Yoshiko?"

She looked at him with disdain.

"I thought we were talking about cats."

"Hm? Yes, so we were. I said women were like cats, Chinese cats."

"Chinese cats are the most vicious!" She made a frightening face, all bared fangs and swatting claws. "They'd rather eat their newborn kittens than let anyone else do so much as touch them!"

"Really? They must have a lot of guts," he said in mock surprise; but there was also a subtle threat in his voice, as if he were again testing her.

Uno's remark sent Yoshiko into a fit of laughter, and she threw back her head, her entire body shaking with mirth.

"Daddy! Do you think I'm like a cat?" She giggled. "Do you?"

She drained her glass in one gulp.

What was she living for? A nation? And if so, what nation? Like someone caught between opposing sides in a tug-of-war, she was doomed to come up empty-handed. But cozying up to one side wasn't any good either. Sometimes she really did hate China. The flag of Manchukuo, with its multicolored stripes, was supposed to symbolize the harmony among the nation's five races—Chinese, Manchu, Mongolian, Muslim, and Tibetan. But what was a flag except for a limp piece of cloth that couldn't even stand up on its own? Ching Empire, indeed! What a farce! The so-called empire was just another Japanese colony. Yoshiko dreamed of dying in battle and going to heaven, where she could command both Japan and Manchukuo from on high. Reality was much harsher—she was just a caged animal, a caged cat.

"You'd best get back and take care of that business," Uno said meaningfully.

Yoshiko faced Yun Kai with mixed feelings, for she knew she could no longer hold him.

His brief convalescence left him thinner and more angular, with prominent cheekbones and brows. While a few days of treatment by a good doctor had healed his wounds, his face remained pallid beneath a blue-black stubble. His grim expression and weary air made it seem as though he bore the suffering of the nation on his young shoulders.

In better times, he might have remained an actor, a Monkey King, somersaulting into middle age until he opened his own studio and took in students, passing the secrets of his art on to another generation. On the other hand, he would have been dead right now if Yoshiko's shot had struck higher.

"I want to leave," he was telling her.

Yoshiko sat down with a flounce.

"Who said you had permission to leave?" Yun Kai was taken aback. The old hard expression returned to her face—or was it just a mask she wore to hide her true feelings?

"Sit down!" she commanded with a theatrical air. "Your organization is in bad shape—workers and college students have been arrested in droves. The minute you walk out the door, you'll be signing your own death warrant."

"What makes you think I'd want to hide out here?" he demanded. "Only a coward would do that!"

Yoshiko sneered. Deciding to change her tack, she assumed the tone of voice she used for interrogations.

"What do you mean 'hide'? You're not hiding from anyone here—you are my prisoner. I am your interrogator, and you'd better get that straight!

"Sit down!" she repeated. "If you don't, I'm going to have to keep on craning my neck to talk to you."

He sat down heavily.

"I have nothing to say. I will never betray my countrymen!"

"Actually, what I had in mind was telling you to disband your little organization. You and your friends are trying to use eggs to break boulders—you overestimate yourselves." She seemed to mull it over. "Besides, I'm your countrywoman, too, am I not?"

By way of demonstration, she walked over to the small altar where she kept the ancestral tablets and where she paid tribute to her illustrious forefathers. Her family name, "Aisin-Gioro," was written in her own hand. She pointed to the altar, hoping he would understand.

"I have never even for a minute forgotten that I am a member of the Ching imperial family, and that I am Chinese. We were born of the same root, you and I. We should work together, not at cross-purposes."

Yun Kai didn't see it that way at all.

"You are a killer of Chinese!" he said angrily.

She bowed her head, thinking. His intractable attitude was getting to be more than she could bear. Those Chinese refused to understand her, and she hated them for it.

"In times of conflict, it is unavoidable that a few drops of blood will be spilled," she said bitterly. "And in the long run, what does it matter? Think about it: What does China have? Money? No! Modern weapons? No! The only thing that China has is so many people, they can't even be counted. And most of them have neither ability nor ambition. Life is cheap. What does it matter if a bunch of them die, especially when those deaths will buy hundreds, perhaps thousands, of years of peace and stability? I'd say it was worth it. That's one of the lessons of history."

"You think you're so clever!" he said scornfully. "If you're so smart, why don't you see that the Japanese are just using you to further their own aims?"

"It might seem that way to someone who is interested only in appearances," she sneered. "Just wait until the game is over, and then you'll see who's been using whom!"

Yun Kai was just a boy who had spent his whole life in the make-believe world of the theater—who could expect him to understand the intricacies of politics? He was strong but simple—all he knew was that Chinese were too busy killing Chinese to notice that a foreign army was taking over their native land, and it filled him with sorrow.

"There's an old saying: 'A loyal minister can't serve two masters.' I never went to school, but I learned a lot from the plays I act in. I know about loyalty, integrity, and respect for one's elders. Loyalty and integrity give a man courage, and they're the hallmarks of true patriotism."

"Hey, not a bad speech! You're a good student. But what you say only proves my point—the Chinese are slaves at heart, what with all their talk of 'loyalty.' The Chinese haven't changed a bit in thousands of years—they always have to have an emperor to tell them what to do. These days it's the Nationalists versus the Communists, but don't let it fool you—they're all the same. All that any of their leaders really wants is to be emperor, to be the savior who rights all the world's wrongs."

"That's not what the students I know say."

"Students? What students?" She shot him a quick look. "They've all been executed!"

Yun Kai felt as though he'd been punched in the stomach, but he leapt to his feet.

"Executed?" His ashen face was suddenly flooded with color. They were his comrades in arms. Bound together by their hatred of a common enemy, they had marched hand in hand, side by side. He would have laid down his own life at a moment's notice—but they needed to live! Unbidden tears streamed down his face.

"You're the only one who's still alive," Yoshiko said icily.

She had rescued him from the jaws of death, but he didn't feel grateful in the least.

"Why kill college students?" he sobbed in anguish. "They had education—they were worth much more than someone like me. If it would bring them back, I'd have you kill me right now!"

He paused.

"I swear I'll fight you to the death!" he spat.

Yoshiko's heart sank, but disappointment soon gave way to anger, as her temper reached the boiling point. All her efforts on his behalf had been wasted!

"I know a brave man when I see one," she said with barely suppressed rage. "Courage is a virtue I value highly—which is why I had you freed. Yet you are still my enemy? Who do you think you are?"

He stood up proudly and faced her. When he spoke, there was not a trace of gratitude in his voice.

"So I owe you my life. Take it back, if you want it! It's yours!" He stared at her levelly, speaking slowly and clearly, as though making a vow: "As long as I draw breath, I shall be your enemy!"

He dropped his head and walked out.

"Halt!" she shouted after him. The gun was in her hand, and she was aiming it squarely at Yun Kai.

He stopped in his tracks and turned to find himself staring straight down the barrel of a gun. She had shot him once before—he knew she wasn't stingy with bullets. He hesitated only a moment before recovering his courage. With one last glance at her, he turned and headed toward the door, still limping a little on his injured leg. He walked with his head held high; the gun sights were trained on the center of his back. One step, two steps, three steps. He wasn't afraid to die.

A shot rang out.

He stopped and closed his eyes, frozen in place. When he opened his eyes again, he realized that the bullet had whizzed past his ear, singeing his hair.

She could have killed him if she'd wanted to, but she let him go.

Yun Kai spoke without turning around, politely but coldly: "Thank you, Commander Chin!"

He strode out. He was really leaving—this time it was forever.

Yoshiko couldn't understand her sudden weakness. Was she shaken by his calmness in the face of death? He acted as though he didn't care whether he lived or died—so maybe it was respect that stayed her hand. It occurred to her that she'd never met anyone as pure and uncomplicated as he was. Then again, perhaps there was more to him than met the eye. After all, when she compared herself to him, he was the one who accomplished what he intended to, while she was left empty-handed.

She felt ashamed. Where was her life headed? The house of cards she spent years trying to prop up had come tumbling down. All at once she felt very old. The eyes that once sparkled with vitality were dim, for the hardships of her life had taken their toll, and she was worn out. After toiling away the best years of her life, she, Hsien-tzu Aisin-Gioro, was just another wounded soldier, her body too crippled even for one last mission.

She had lost him! He was gone from her life forever.

She crumpled to the floor, but then, like a woman possessed, she began firing wildly at the walls around her. Glass shattered, crystal lamps jingled, and then everything went dark as one of the bullets knocked out the last light bulb. The floor was strewn with wreckage, the bits and pieces of a life that could never be made whole again. A chilling vision of the future rose up before her eyes: The strongmen of Japanese militarism were taking up their brooms and sweeping it all away, tossing these fragments of her soul onto the dust heap of history.

Japan's invasion of China was official now, and the Kwantung Army no longer needed to mask its intentions—Yoshiko was no longer an asset. They didn't need her anymore.

Manchukuo was just a stepping-stone.

At 11:00 P.M. on the evening of July 7, 1937, the Japanese Army unit garrisoned at Fengtai, a suburb of Peking, went on night exercises near the Marco Polo Bridge. Claiming that an infantryman had been lost during maneuvers, the commanding officers demanded entry to the nearby walled town of Wanping in order to search for him and, on this pretext, bombarded the town. Reinforcements arrived, and soon Peking was surrounded on three sides; the city's Nationalist government, unable to get aid from General Chiang Kai-shek, was forced to retreat in the face of this massive offensive. Peking fell, and Tientsin fell with it.

Japanese planes started bombing Shanghai, indiscriminately and around the clock. Bombs fell on the Bund and on Shanghai's thriving downtown commercial district until an area of several square miles was reduced to rubble. Not one roof tile lay unbroken, and the ground was littered with corpses.

After the fall of Shanghai, the Japanese Army marched on to Nanking, where it began a bloody six-week massacre. No one was spared in that orgy of murder, rape, looting, and destruction. In Nanking alone, the dead and wounded numbered more than three hundred thousand. The Nationalist government abandoned the city, and the Japanese boldly announced that China would be laid waste within three months.

From there, the Japanese turned south, implementing a policy called the "Three Everythings": burn everything, kill everything, steal everything. All of China was plunged into terror and despair. Chinese were no better than dogs, and if a Chinese citizen did not bow down low enough for Japan's imperial soldiers, he could easily lose his life.

Yoshiko was no longer at the center of the action, but she struggled to keep up the appearance of power and influence, bringing in a little cash by extorting money from defenseless shopkeepers or selling occasional bits of information to the Japanese military, and trying hard to curry favor with Madam Hideki Tojo, the wife of Japan's prime minister. But she was living on borrowed time.

Meanwhile, a Nationalist official named Wang Ching-wei fled the Nationalist stronghold of Chungking for British-controlled Hong Kong, where he issued a cease-fire declaration. Wang then set up a new "Nationalist government" in Nanking, in 1940, and the rival Chungking and Nanking governments were plunged in bitter strife. Soon the Communists joined in the fray.

With China's rulers embroiled in internal conflict, conditions for her 400 million people, most of whom wanted nothing more from life than a full belly and a roof over their heads, went from bad to worse. Many people became professional refugees. Some managed to escape; most did not.

One day Kwantung Army Headquarters received the following message:

Your subordinate Shunkichi Uno reports on the status of Yoshiko Kawashima as follows. The Pacification Army under her has been disbanded, and, while Yoshiko was extremely effective at one time and helped our noble emperor's forces to achieve many victories, she is no longer useful. Moreover, she has become a liability, having acted on her own to free an anti-Japanese guerrilla for purely personal reasons. She is no longer reliable, and we request permission to issue a top-secret order for her termination.

The higher-ups granted Uno's request, and the orders were conveyed to a skilled and experienced operative. Up to now, this man had been involved in propaganda work, directing much of the cultural life of the new state of Manchukuo and establishing a national film studio there. As studio chief, he found an obscure young Japanese girl named Yoshiko Yamaguchi, and, with a little bit of tinkering, made her over into a Chinese actress named Li Hsiang-lan—Fragrant Orchid. He promoted her aggressively, and she starred in quite a few movies, to the great benefit of Japanese-Manchurian friendship and interracial harmony. But if he was famous for his movies, his real work was in military intelligence. His name was Yamaga.

He felt more than a bit rattled when he received his orders at headquarters. They were putting him in a very awkward position. Why had they chosen him?

19

It was midafternoon—the clock read 3:20—and Yoshiko was still asleep. Her face still bore traces of last night's makeup, a smudge of powder and faded eyeshadow, a half-painted mouth. She had gone straight to bed without bothering to wash any of it off, like a tired clown.

Tossing and turning, she dreamed strange dreams, her face alternately twitching and relaxing into a calm expression. Then, as if touched by a ghost, she awoke with a start.

A man's shadow fell across the foot of the bed. He had his back to the light, and she couldn't make out his face. Suddenly, she recognized him and all but jumped out of her skin—it was Yamaga, her first love. Wasn't it long over between them? she wondered. What was he doing in her bedroom?

He couldn't bring himself to do what he had been sent to do. She lay silently on the bed, worn and haggard. The passing illusions of beauty and youth were gone, leaving nothing behind but this pitiful heap of flesh and bones. Her vitality and her looks were irretrievably gone—her eyes had lost their luster, her hair its body. Coughing twice in rapid succession, she tried to sit up.

"You!" she hissed, collapsing back onto the bed. "What are you doing here?"

Yamaga didn't respond. His gaze fell upon the morphine needle on the nightstand.

"It's been a long time," Yoshiko pressed. "Don't tell me you just happened to be in the neighborhood and felt like dropping in! Who sent you?"

Her nerves were on edge, but she tried to compose herself.

He went to the window and opened the curtains. A shaft of sunlight, filled with dancing motes of dust, reached out toward her. She squinted into the strong light.

"I merely came to see how you were doing. You needn't be suspicious."

She laughed harshly.

"When you're in my line of work, you learn to be careful. I wouldn't be alive if I weren't suspicious. Why should you be any exception?"

She knew what kind of man he was; he had no illusions about her, either. Only fate could decide the outcome of this game. Years ago, in the beginning, when they were young and deeply in love, they would never have deceived one another. Now, they were like a pair of scorpions facing off.

"Pull yourself together, Yoshiko! Isn't that the advice you once gave me?"

She had all but forgotten that letter, those words, the thousand yen. Her life had become an endless journey. Only fate can decide, she told him then. Pull yourself together!

"Get up," he said curtly, "and put on some nice clothes. Let's get some fresh air."

She stared at him fixedly for some time before she got out of her high, cushioned bed and went to the bathroom to wash up. She purposefully left the bathroom door ajar as a way of showing her trust. As she washed her face, she speculated as to why he was there. The water coming out the tap was muddy— she wasn't sure if it was rust or a broken pipe, but the water was full of tiny particles. The water in China was never clear.

Yamaga hesitated outside the door. He knew why she left the door open, and it made his task all the harder.

Yoshiko spoke to him from inside the bathroom.

"If you came here on some particular business," she hinted, "then don't let me stand in your way! Still, I want you to know that it is a privilege to be with my first love—"

She emerged from the bathroom, drying her hair with a large towel. She glanced at him in the mirror and smiled.

"Yoshiko," he said. "Would you dress yourself up the way you used to and just let me look at you for a while?"

She turned to face him.

"Those whose lives are mostly behind them are the ones who like to reminisce," she said pleasantly. "I have quite a few years ahead of me yet, and many things left to do."

"For instance?"

"Off hand, I can't really say. Success? Love? A family? Friends? Power? Money? Justice? They're all illusions. None of them really matter."

"How about peace?" Yamaga asked softly.

"If you ask me, that's the biggest sham of all! Come on, let's go out for a bit."

Yamaga was having second thoughts.

Nervously, Yoshiko opened her closet and started going through her clothes, at last deciding on one of her cheongsams. It was one big gamble, she thought to herself. She was trying everything, but she couldn't figure him out.

"Did you know," she said softly, "that when a woman succeeds, it's because a man has been propping her up? Women are only bad because men worship them blindly. Sometimes I think we women can only be at peace in a world without men." It was like a *cri de coeur*—she was talking more to herself than to him.

At last she slipped her arm through his and announced that she was ready.

"Let's go," she said.

She took a great deal of care with her appearance, hiding her worn and tired features underneath a blanket of paints and powders; but it was all an illusion. Beneath that lovely surface, she was just as haggard as ever. Still, her beauty now dazzled him.

A rickshaw brought the pair up to the entrance to a Taoist temple. They got out and ascended the temple steps one at a time. Yoshiko was still holding him companionably, seemingly free of all fear and suspicion.

Looking up, Yamaga read the plaque over the lintel: SIX HARMONIES. He noticed the scent of incense and reflected that, even in these most troubled of times, the temple was an oasis of calm where nothing changed. A couplet hung beside the door to the shrine:

Spread the word—benighted souls will follow the path to
enlightenment.

Show the Way—mankind will open the gates of the world
to the kingdom of heaven.

Some people still believed that everything was preordained,
and that one simply had to surrender to fate.

The hall was filled with memorial shrines inscribed with the
names of the departed: Madam Wang, Master Li, and all the other
esteemed ancestors of the faithful. YOUR VOICE AND VISAGE ARE
WITH US STILL, read one plaque, beneath which were offerings of
gladioli, roses, yellow chrysanthemums, fruits, cakes, and other
sweets.

The fragrance of sandalwood incense drifted through the air.

"It's a funny thing." Yoshiko sighed with deep feeling. "As
long as we're alive, we're worthless. We only become precious
after we die."

"Go ahead. Light some incense," he urged.

"What about you?"

He shook his head.

"I'm not a believer."

She lit her incense and turned her back to him, murmuring,
". . . but I believe."

Yamaga's hand went involuntarily to the revolver at his
waist. He had his orders.

In one corner of the temple, a medium was telling fortunes
by writing characters in fine sand spread over a board. When the
spirit entered him, he started to write, his brush flying as he traced
the characters, one after another in quick succession, in a dazzling
display. Each one was a mystical diagram that he alone under-

stood, and he read them aloud for his assistant to write down in pen and ink. A woman was seeking a prescription, and the medium recited a long list of Chinese herbs:

"We have sought a remedy for cataracts of the left eye. The prescription is five ounces of *shu-ti,* three ounces of *chuan-lien,* three ounces of *niu-chi,* three ounces of *huai-shan,* a half ounce of *ju-hsiang* . . ."

When he finished, the woman knelt down respectfully and kowtowed in deep gratitude. Then she left, prescription in hand.

"Something bothering you?" Yoshiko prodded Yamaga. "Go ahead. Have him tell your fortune."

"I don't have any particular question to ask him."

"Well, just ask him about your future in general," she persisted. She glanced at him, trying to read his heart.

"All right." He nodded and turned to the medium. "I'd like to know whether or not I can accomplish my task. My surname is Wang."

The diviner's brush started to move, and as he wrote, he intoned:

"Mr. Wang would like to know whether or not he can complete his task. He was born in 1894, in the Year of the Horse, and is noble in appearance."

The answer came right away:

"In ten years, he will die miserably because of a woman. He will commit suicide, his body left in the wilderness to be eaten by wild dogs. But, if he can avoid this disaster, his luck will change, and he will know untold riches."

When he heard this, Yamaga broke into a cold sweat. It was as though someone had dumped a bucket of freezing water over his head. He didn't know if he believed what he heard or not. Did these Chinese ghosts really have the power and wisdom to guide him? What did it mean—in ten years he would die because of a woman? They were at an impasse. One of them would have to die, and the choice was his.

He was over forty years old, a man of the world. Should he believe or not? He didn't notice Yoshiko walking over to stand behind him in silent witness to his inner turmoil. He was conscious of nothing but one question: Should he believe or not?

Yamaga turned around to face her squarely and unconsciously dropped back a step to see her more clearly. He would accept what fate offered him. Perhaps the spirits read his mind and were merely spelling out the decision he had already made on his own. Deep down, he knew that he could not bring himself to kill her.

"Yoshiko," he said, but he didn't need to say anything— they both knew. "I'll see to it that you return to Japan!"

Was he letting her go? A shadow of suspicion flickered across Yoshiko's face. Did he mean it?

The lonely quay on a harbor outside of Tientsin was deserted except for the two of them. As Yamaga helped Yoshiko with her luggage, she was looking all around, not daring to believe he would really let her go. Past experience taught her not to trust anyone, least of all those closest to her: The gentlest person often turned out to be a cold-blooded killer. And she should know. Was she about to get her comeuppance for all of her betrayals?

With every move he made, she grew more wary, her eyes bright. Was he trying to lull her into letting her guard down so that he could spring on her later? Was he finally going to make his move here in this desolate, godforsaken place? Or did he really mean what he said? Was that possible in a world like this?

Yamaga put his hand in his pocket, and Yoshiko's heart pounded with terror. Her life hung by a thread. She knew only too well that in the past she had abused and insulted the one man who could save her now. She couldn't pretend to be in love with him anymore—still, she once called him her own. But that was a long time ago, when they were in love. Did he remember?

He pulled a roll of bills from his pocket—Japanese yen—and with great care put the money into her handbag. She looked up at him, ashamed of her own suspicions and suddenly filled with self-loathing. What could she say to him?

"Sometimes those fortune-tellers are right. Are you sure you won't reconsider?"

He laughed and shook his head.

"I don't believe in any of that stuff. Your boat's here. Take care of yourself!"

She boarded the barge, which took her out to the mail ship that would carry her to Japan. He had arranged her escape in secret. It was no luxury cruise, but he was giving her another chance, a chance to start all over again. She would have to lie low for a while.

As he waved to her from the dock, she knew she would probably never see him again, this man who had the sense of justice to save her just when she thought she had reached the end. She felt grateful. He had so much integrity he didn't even embrace her in farewell.

She boarded the ship. The China Sea now separated them. In another ironic twist of fate, the Chinese woman was fleeing to Japan, while the Japanese man stayed on Chinese soil.

Yamaga turned resolutely and left without looking back, his feelings well hidden.

Yoshiko stood motionless, her eyes filled with tears. How

transient our lives are, she mused. Youth and beauty fade away like the delicate fragrance of spring flowers; all that is good and beautiful seems doomed to wither.

Throughout her voyage, a tune kept going through her head, so faintly that she couldn't be sure whether there was a radio somewhere on board ship, or if it was just a trick of her memory. It shadowed her like a wandering ghost, and she couldn't shake it off. Who was the singer? Was it Li Hsiang-lan or Hamako Watanabe? The song had a haunting quality, filled with a passionate tremulousness:

> China night, oh China night,
> Harbor lights in the violet night . . .

Ten years, she thought. Ten glorious years.

> I dream of spring, I dream of you:
> The sun shining high in the sky,
> Roses blazing bright as fire,
> When we meet by the riverside.
> But I awaken and you are gone.
> Oh, spring dream, dream of love.

Those years were like a dream from which she awakened empty-handed, a failure. She had sacrificed everything over the past ten years, giving and giving until she was bled dry. She felt like a dying sun sinking west over the wilderness, glowing for one last moment before it sinks forever into the abyss. Still, she believed she had her "nation," although, in truth, there was no place she could really call home. She didn't even have a place to rest her tired head.

20

It was spring again, late March in Tokyo. Billowing pink clouds of cherry blossoms spread like a giant canopy over the hills and parks of the city. The sky, normally rumbling with bombers, was quiet today and completely cloudless. It looked like a thin piece of silk, decorated with layer upon layer of pale pink petals, and touched with the delicately sweet but vaguely melancholy fragrance of face powder.

Yoshiko was dressed rather carelessly in a man's kimono. A sloppily knotted blue sash sagged lopsidedly across her hips. She lolled on her back in a grove of stubby trees, one knee bent up, the rest of her body limp. Several empty sake bottles lay off to the side, sprawling drunkenly like their mistress, who squinted up toward the clear and perfumed heavens. The masses of petals looked as though they had been daubed on by some mad finger painter.

The cherry blossoms bloom first in the south and then travel slowly northward up the length of the island nation, taking about a month in all from the start of the cherry season to its end. Every year it is the same—the profusion of flowers dazzles the eyes, but only for a brief moment. In the blink of an eye, the stunning display is replaced by a scene of desolation.

Yoshiko had drunk a great deal of sake and felt about ready to burst—she urgently needed to relieve herself. There was no one there for her to impress with her beauty or refinement, she told herself. Wasn't she just like anyone else? Anyway, trying to impress other people was a stupid waste of time, she concluded, and pulled herself up into the thin branches of a cherry tree. Squatting there as she prepared to relieve herself, she honestly didn't care if anyone was watching or not, although as it turned out the park was all but deserted on this particular afternoon. She lifted up the hem of her kimono and started to urinate. As it trickled to the ground, an unpleasantly pungent odor rose into the air.

A little monkey nimbly sprang away from the rank-smelling patch of grass, although he didn't go very far before he turned around to wink mischievously at his mistress with his tiny bright eyes. Yoshiko was well on her way to being completely drunk, and she clumsily clambered down out of the tree, grinning at her monkey. She collapsed into a heap on the grass, arms and legs flung out every which way, not wanting to get up.

The monkey sauntered agilely over to her side. She had tamed him until he seemed almost human to her.

"Ah-fu," she mumbled. "You're the only friend I have, anymore!"

Ah-fu scratched his cheeks quizzically and opened his eyes so wide that they looked like little saucers. He had a very expressive face, but he never smiled, even when he was beside himself with joy. Not even the dimple of a smile ever touched his face. Only people can smile, although they smile far too rarely.

Yoshiko was smiling to herself just then, as a breath of spring breeze puffed by and cherry blossoms rained down on her, covering her chest with crimson tears. The flowers were dying already, giving up their brief and wistful lives.

As the sun sank slowly, somebody walked up to where Yoshiko lay. It was Naniwa Kawashima. His thin silhouette was like a skeleton, as he leaned on his staff in the dying light, a very old man.

Yoshiko opened her eyes and saw his shadow stretching across the grass. She didn't want to see him. Still, every other man she'd ever known had drifted away, and he was still there! Life was strange, indeed. The only man still at her side was the one she hated the most, the one whom she had tried with all her might to wash from her memory, scrubbing so hard sometimes she bled.

He was so old and decrepit that it seemed almost inconceivable that long ago he was a lean and vigorous activist and thinker, a central figure in the Manchurian-Mongolian Independence Movement, a man of great ambition, a crafty and slippery operator. Even he, once as hard as steel, couldn't resist the predations of time. He was as doomed to wither as the fragile cherry blossoms. At any moment, he could be trampled underfoot, ground into the mud, unnoticed and unmourned.

Yoshiko recognized that she was no different from him in this respect—but that recognition was quickly followed by denial. She refused to believe it, but it was there, right before her eyes. She shut her eyes tight, wanting to block it all out. Kawashima turned toward the setting sun, and she thought she heard him moaning, low and sorrowful, on the wind:

"Human beings are as fragile as glass. Just one tiny touch, and we shatter to bits, irreparable. . . ."

Yoshiko climbed up out of the mass of crushed petals to stagger home. Ah-fu hopped onto her shoulder, needing her as much as she needed him. He was like family to her, her most intimate and beloved companion. She didn't trust people anymore—he alone was dependable. When she poured her heart out to him, he always listened attentively, not missing a thing. He was the guardian of her soul, which she had given him a piece at a time, until the pieces came together and formed the image of a woman of great courage and nobility, capable of great things but born at the wrong time. This was the story she told him, and he seemed to believe her. She loved him deeply, without fear, knowing he would never turn on her. His sharp, animal odor filled her lungs as she breathed in.

Cherry blossoms gave way to wisteria, those harbingers of summer. These in turn gave way to the red leaves of autumn, which blazed on the hills for weeks on end, more beautiful than any flowers. Yoshiko's monkey became slightly ill, and she took him up to the hills, where she let him loose to find the medicinal grasses he needed to cure himself.

Winter arrived, and fine snow dusted the earth like pure white face powder. Yoshiko was reclining, completely naked and up to her chest in the steaming water of a hot spring. Snowflakes were sifting down in endless spirals, only to be instantly annihilated in the scalding water.

Yoshiko bowed her head and regarded her frail body. Her bones were plainly visible, although she hadn't grown so thin that they stuck out too sharply. Her skin was still pale and unblemished, but not her hands. A woman's hands can never lie, least of all to the woman herself. Blue veins snaked over the backs of her hands, looking like faded indigo dye printed on white cloth. With the blood of so many people on them, it seemed odd that all that remained now was a bleached blue and white.

She was thirty-six years old. Half of her life was behind her, but it wasn't over yet. How long did she have? she wondered.

Her breasts, still small and perfectly shaped, floated half-submerged in the water, the tiny red mole bobbing as if on an invisible string. It was still the same blood-red teardrop that had undone so many men. Was she ruined as well? Were there no more great missions for her to carry out? Would she live out the rest of her days like this?

Yoshiko caught a glimpse of her own tired and ravaged face reflected on the surface of the water. Even a flower had to bloom brightly until the end, before it could earn the right to bow out gracefully. After her return to Tokyo, what had she done but hide herself away in her room day and night, idling away the months without purpose? In the spring, she climbed the hills to admire the flowers, and in the winter she rode the train up to the hot springs. It was an aimless and dispirited existence. Would her remaining days be one long, slow death? Was Princess Hsien-tzu, the fourteenth daughter of Prince Su, just an ordinary woman in the vast sea of humanity?

Never! Yoshiko leapt up suddenly, naked from head to toe, and dashed off, water streaming off her body. At the inn, Ah-fu, the monkey, watched her uncomprehendingly as she made a phone call, still stark naked and too full of feverish energy even to throw on a robe.

The person she was phoning was Katsuko Tojo, the wife of Japan's prime minister, Hideki Tojo. At one time, she and Yoshiko were quite close—Yoshiko avidly courted her friendship, and the two became very familiar.

If Yoshiko were to come out of retirement, she needed to find a backer. It was 1943, and the Pacific War was at a height, with U.S.-Japanese relations at an all-time low. The Japanese people were tasting the bitter fruit of a war waged against themselves, while China's long-suffering masses struggled to survive in their war-torn homeland. Yoshiko could claim either nation as her "homeland." She wished with all her heart for an end to the fighting and dreamed of a day when Japan and China would be united. If only she had wings to fly back to China on a mission of peace and speak to General Chiang Kai-shek. She honestly believed she could convince him if given the chance.

She waited for the operator to put her call through. At last Katsuko answered.

"Madam Tojo," she said hopefully. "This is Yoshiko—do you remember me?"

There was silence on the other end.

"It's Yoshiko," she said more urgently, her heart pounding. "I know it's been a long time since we last saw each other. . . . Yes, that's right. Yes . . . I'd like to return to China. Sino-Japanese peace talks can't go forward without an intermediary, and since I'm quite familiar with the Nationalist government, I'm confident that I— Oh, no. I never said I'd retired. . . ."

Although the woman on the other end of the line treated her perfunctorily, Yoshiko was riding high on a wave of self-confidence and didn't even notice the other woman's indifference. She plunged on, headlong, in a final, desperate attempt to sell herself.

"Please, just give me this one last chance! Tell Mr. Tojo, and send me—"

A loud buzzing sound in the receiver told her she had been cut off.

"Hello? Madam Tojo?"

Nobody was interested in Yoshiko anymore. Nobody.

Even if Tojo were interested in using Yoshiko (which he wasn't), he certainly wouldn't have been interested in her proposal. The great general Hideki Tojo had no intention whatsoever of holding any kind of peace talks. Japan's mission was to establish the Greater East Asia Coprosperity Sphere by bringing China, Hong Kong, Singapore, Malaysia, Siam, and all the rest of Asia under its control. From there, it would branch out to control the entire world.

Yoshiko Kawashima was just a pawn on this world political chessboard. It didn't matter to her masters whether she lived or died, but they had let her live, and now she was scoffing at their generosity by meddling in matters that didn't concern her. Her feelings were like wild horses—once they were let loose to run, they galloped away, out of control. She would stop at nothing to get what she wanted. She hadn't changed at all. Maybe it was something in her blood, a fatal flaw with which she was born. She could easily live out the rest of her life quietly, forgetting her past and keeping to herself. But she couldn't fight her nature. Unable to break free, unable to run away, she was bound to history. She couldn't forget who she was or what she had done. She hurled herself back into the web, unable or unwilling to accept that she was out of her depth.

Yoshiko booked passage on a ship bound for China. One day, dressed in a cheongsam, dark glasses, and a scarf that whipped in the cutting wind, she came to Tung–hsing Lou, her old Tientsin stomping ground.

It was in ruins. The big sign that once hung so proudly from the front of the building was just a broken old board; the building itself was a mere heap of rubble. Crumbled bricks and broken tiles, some bearing traces of bloodstains, were all that remained of the once-imposing restaurant. It was absurd even to think of rebuilding it.

This was the monkey's first time in these strange surroundings. He crouched warily on her shoulder, hardly daring to move as he stared, wide-eyed, at the desolation around him.

Picking up her suitcases, Yoshiko started walking down the street. Even with Ah-fu as a companion, she was still alone. Where could she go? She might as well go to Peking.

As she walked along, deep in thought, a crude voice stopped her short.

"Hey! You!" the voice yelled. "Bow when you see a soldier of the Imperial Army!"

Trembling with suppressed rage, she stood stubbornly, rooted to the ground. Was this to be the fruit of her labors, the only repayment for her sacrifices?

Slowly, ever so slowly, she took off her dark glasses and looked the cocky young Japanese soldier right in the eye. He was very young, a new enlistee, one of the men brought in to replace the previous generation. She faced him mutely for a long while. It was a standoff. He was determined to see her bow, but she didn't budge.

At last Yoshiko spoke, her voice weary but firm and clear: "Do you realize who I am?"

21

"Do you realize who I am?"

The words echoed in the packed courtroom, weary but firm. As arrogant as ever, Yoshiko seemed to be looking down her nose at all present. They were beneath her notice. Of course, at that very moment she was a captured spy, a criminal, and worthless in their eyes as well. She had lived a full life, this woman, caught between two nations, two loyalties. Was there truly any crime in that?

Her smile was like ice.

"The people I associated with were all big shots. Are they also being interrogated by a bunch of nobodies like yourselves? I don't know whether to laugh or cry! None of your government officials, even Generalissimo Chiang Kai-shek himself, are my equals!"

The magistrate shifted uncomfortably—at some level what she said was true.

She raised her chin high. Was she throwing down a gauntlet? She was a princess, and she expected to be treated like one. It was lost on her that in comparison to the powerful forces of history, she was nothing.

The magistrate was trying to establish a chronology of her life. He produced a tall stack of photographs, which he placed, one by one, before her. Reading off the names of the people in the pictures, he asked her:

"Do you remember these people now?"

She saw the face of almost every man she had ever known. There were a lot of them. He kept on reciting the names, but she cut him off midsyllable.

"There's no point in your making me look at these things again, Your Honor," she said sarcastically. "I don't know any of these people!"

Next, the judge took out a large pile of documents.

"These depositions all pertain to your tenure as commander in chief of the Pacification Army. Ten prisoners have testified to serving under you. Furthermore, we have written evidence that you once commanded several thousand soldiers, brutally murdered members of the resistance, instigated several bloody riots, and directly or indirectly caused the deaths of countless numbers of your own countrymen."

Seized by a sudden inspiration, she quickly demanded:

"When was all this supposedly going on?"

"Starting in the twentieth year of the Republic—that is, 1931—and continuing for ten years, altogether."

Yoshiko let out a harsh cackle, as though she had just heard a particularly ridiculous joke.

"Ha!" she blurted out. "That's a good one, Your Honor! I was born in Japan in the fifth year of the Taisho reign—that's 1916 to you Chinese. Do you know how to add? In 1931, I was fifteen years old, just a child! How could I have led thousands of soldiers to battle? How could a girl of fifteen do all those horrible things?"

"Why does the accused deliberately falsify her age?" the judge demanded severely. "Is she attempting to conceal her crimes?"

The year was 1946, and anyone could see that Yoshiko was a woman of about forty, haggard and thin, her face lined with wrinkles that could never be erased. Even if she were speaking the truth, nobody would have believed her. She fooled no one but herself—everyone else saw through her little ruse. Sitting behind bars as the evidence of her guilt piled up around her made her desperate—the end of the road was near. She was sinking fast, but still she refused to give up, clutching at any splinter of hope with her last ounce of strength. Even if it was a million to one, she wouldn't let any chance for survival slip by.

Stony-faced, she was refusing to back down.

"You spent an entire year interrogating me, and I never broke down. I couldn't tell you what you wanted to hear. And do you know why? You were wrong about my age from the very beginning!"

"Where is your proof? Do you have any?"

Yoshiko thought for a moment before answering.

"I do indeed. Send to my father, Naniwa Kawashima, in Japan for my household registration papers, and be quick about it! He can attest to the fact that I was only ten years old in 1926,

when you say I was invading China. He can also tell you that
I am Japanese, and not Chinese. You have treated me unfairly and
unjustly, forcing me to fight for my life. But everything will be
put to rights if you contact my father and he remembers what
I am to him."

She gazed levelly at the magistrate as the details of her plan
crystallized in her mind.

"You'll see, Your Honor—once those documents get here,
everyone will realize the big mistake you've made, and I can go
home."

If this didn't work, she would be lost. Perhaps time was on
her side, she thought. At the very least she could try to cheat the
years. If Kawashima had any heart at all, he would lie for her and
testify that she was Japanese—then, even the highest court in the
land could not convict her. She would be free.

Yoshiko was very calm as the guards escorted her back to
her cell in Peking's Municipal Prison Number One.

Long ago, the cell walls had been white, but over the years
they had become stained with dirt and soot mixed in with old
bloodstains. Each cell was thirteen feet high, with a square iron-
barred window facing the central courtyard. There was a wooden
plank for a bed; a bucket in the corner served as a chamber pot.
The light was very dim, as dingy as the prisoners' gray uniforms.

Some cells held as many as three dozen inmates, but Yoshiko
was a problem prisoner and had a cell to herself. The previous
inhabitant, a woman who had murdered her rival in love, had
died in that cell.

There was a small hole at one corner of the cell for passing
food to the prisoner. The prison food consisted of watery soup
and coarse corn bread, but Yoshiko devoured it hungrily.

"When I think of how His Majesty must be suffering in Russia right now," she told herself, "how can I feel too sorry for myself?"

She crouched down and took a bite of bread. It was cold and hard, and when she bit into it, crumbs rained down. When she was in her prime and her power was at its peak, she would never have believed that one day she would be squatting in a place like this, eating things even a dog wouldn't touch. Looking up toward the high barred window, she couldn't see the sky. Someday, she thought, someday I'll see the sky again, and leave this noisy and foul place far behind me!

Noisy it was, indeed. Criminals of every type were there: traitors, murderesses, drug dealers, opium addicts, thieves, grave robbers. Some of these women were beautiful and some ugly, but all were tarred with same brush: They were the dregs of society. Locked up all day, they made a raucous din, wailing and shouting from dawn till dusk, singing, dancing, weeping. It was filthy and it stank, and nobody was given anything with which to wash herself, much less a change of clothes.

Still, Yoshiko thought she was different from the others. They were common, petty criminals, who had never seen the world. None of them had really lived, not the way she had—they were just a bunch of sewer rats, scuttling off into the shadows, hatching their dirty little schemes. They were beneath her notice, the way they squabbled over trifles, sometimes raising a ruckus that lasted all day. Something as worthless as tooth powder was enough to cause a scuffle. Even in prison, Yoshiko still had her dignity, and she was constantly shouting at the others to stop.

"What's all that racket about? You're all so small-minded!"

She swore to herself that if she ever got out of here, she would never come back. She would rather die.

A sentimental love song was playing on someone's radio, and all the inmates fell silent.

"When will my love return?" the singer half cried, like the melancholy ghost of an abandoned woman. Yoshiko drowsily closed her eyes, listening as the song played on, a drug that calmed the prisoners, until bit by bit it grew silent all around. There were only two roads left open to this "Venus in a Suit"—to die in obscurity, or to live on in obscurity.

"Miss Yoshiko!"

Someone was calling to her. She opened her eyes and saw that it was her lawyer. Her heart leapt.

"Mr. Li!"

He had a sheaf of documents with him—the gift she had been awaiting for so long was at last here! Barely able to contain herself, she took a deep breath before opening the file. She quickly skimmed through it, her eyes racing over the lines; but when she reached the end, she went straight back to the beginning and read it more slowly:

"Yoshiko Kawashima is an alias of the Chinese woman known as Chin Pi-hui. She is the fourteenth daughter of Shanchi, Prince Su. I personally had no children of my own, and I adopted Yoshiko when she was six years old at the behest of her family. This took place on October 25, 1913."

Yoshiko's face fell, but she read on.

"Since childhood, most Japanese people have taken her to be a Japanese citizen."

She couldn't believe it. She read it again, clutching the paper tightly as a cold sweat crept over her body. Was this it? Was this the proof of identity she had anxiously awaited day and night? He hadn't even changed her birth year to 1916, nor had he tried to explain that she was really Japanese. It was outrageous! This wasn't what she had asked for at all.

She looked up at Mr. Li with panic-stricken eyes, completely at a loss.

"He didn't do what I asked," she said in a daze. "I didn't want him to tell the truth. I wanted him to lie—to save my life!"

Li was sympathetic but could do nothing to help her.

"In the past, Mr. Kawashima had dealings with the Black Dragon Society, and he is still under surveillance. One slip, and the United Nations will prosecute him as a war criminal. He didn't dare perjure himself, least of all in writing! I'm afraid that his testimony has only worsened your position."

"But he's over eighty. . . ." she said dully.

"If there were anything I could do, I would do it, Miss Yoshiko."

Her face went ashen as she slumped into a dejected heap. He was her last hope—and now that hope had been destroyed. It was like falling into a glacial crevasse. She clutched the letter with stiff and icy hands. Was there any way out now? She didn't want to die. He was her first, she reflected, moaning in disbelief.

"It's funny," she said hoarsely. "That man spent his entire life telling lies—what made him decide to start telling the truth all of a sudden? I don't understand it."

She seemed to wilt. Her arms drooped limply at her sides as the papers slipped through her fingers, like her ebbing life.

At eleven-fifteen on the morning of October 22, 1947, the magistrate read Yoshiko's sentence:

"You, Chin Pi-hui, known also by the Japanese alias of Yoshiko Kawashima, having been found guilty of committing the crimes of treason and espionage, are to be stripped of your civil rights as well as all of your personal property for the rest of your natural life. This court further sentences you to death."

His voice was flat and unemotional, and she listened, dull-eyed. The crowd whooped with joy as a silent Yoshiko was escorted back to the prison, her frail figure disappearing into its depths. The blocks of cells seemed to stretch on forever—she knew there was no escape. The sounds of clapping and shouting grew fainter and fainter, stopping abruptly as the prison doors slammed behind her.

Memories of Peking in the springtime came flooding back to her. It was a time when pale green foliage adorned the city walls, and an array of blossoms—lilac, forsythia, apricot, cherry, peach—held the old capital in a fragrant embrace, while the crimson pillars and marble steps of the Forbidden City were bathed in the golden light of sunset. How beautiful Peking was, at any time of day, in any season. Yoshiko wondered if she would live to see another spring. Would she even see the new year? It was unimaginable, but she might not see another springtime. Like a butterfly who has lost its wings, she had not only lost the ability to fly, she had lost her beauty as well.

Locked up in prison, she grew thin and hollow-eyed, and one of her front teeth fell out. Lack of sunlight left her skin papery white, and she grew so emaciated she seemed lost in her baggy gray uniform. Fate was battering her, persistently and intensely, like storm waves battering the shore, until she became so worn down she no longer cared.

One day, she saw something that briefly shook her out of her apathy. She thought she saw a prisoner who resembled Shun-kichi Uno being led into the prison. Could that criminal shuffling along with a bowed head really be him? Maybe there was some justice in the world after all.

She lifted up her bowl of coarse noodle soup and slurped noisily, down to the very last drop of broth. When there was nothing left, she let out a great belch. Now that her belly was full, she turned her attention to satisfying another pressing need and gave herself a shot of morphine. Letting her head loll back, she sighed contentedly, enveloped in a warm and peaceful haze. Leaning against the wall, she looked like nothing so much as a heap of dirty rags. She had given up; and yet, in giving up, she seemed to find some solace.

The other women inmates were filled with pity when they learned of Yoshiko's death sentence, and many of them wept for her; despite their violent natures, these women were not without humanity. True, many had murdered their husbands or committed crimes even more shocking, but they shared something in common with Yoshiko—she, like them, was only in prison because of men! She would have been the first to admit it, too; anyone passing by her cell during the day might have heard her muttering to herself, "I despise men!"

When she saw the others crying for her, she pretended not to know why.

She needed a postage stamp and pulled a wad of bills from her purse, handing them over to the warden.

"Twenty-five thousand yuan?" she asked.

"No, thirty thousand."

She didn't have much choice and paid up. Paper was expensive, too—everything in prison was expensive, for that matter—and she bent her head over her letter, writing in tiny, cramped characters, trying to fit as much as she could onto one scrap of paper. She was writing to a man—a man she finally forgave.

To my respected Father, it began. *Happy New Year!*

She called him "Father" still. She had only known her natural father until the age of seven and had only the haziest impressions of him. It was the foster father who raised her who

actually changed her life. But maybe it wasn't so one-sided—
didn't she also change the lives of many men?

What was the point of thinking about it? She was reaching
the end of the line. She wrote on:

I haven't got much time left. I feel like the withered flowers
and dead leaves left behind by the autumn wind—at least
I once knew the glory of springtime. I had my day, and as
long as one can say one did something useful in life, then
one needn't have any regrets.

In many ways, prison is a kind of paradise, a safe place
where nobody has to work, but everybody has food to eat.
It's not such a bad life, really!

I do have a few complaints, however. I've heard that
the papers are suggesting I be turned into some kind of
tent-show attraction, with the proceeds from ticket sales
being donated to charity. Speculators have adapted my story
to musicals, without so much as asking my permission. It's
incredibly disrespectful!

Of course, there is something ennobling about impending death. One becomes quite magnanimous and ceases
to be troubled by little things like these. One no longer
cares. I know that I am going to die and that there's nothing
I can do about it. So I might as well tell the world that I
don't have any more secrets to tell, least of all about others.
Nothing can save me now, so I might as well assume the
guilt for everybody else's crimes, too, and save them the
misery. Why should I add to the world's suffering?

Nobody visits me or brings me gifts. The people I used
to know here in prison have all turned their backs on me;
but it doesn't matter anymore. Close friendships are too
risky, anyway.

When life becomes truly terrible, there's nothing one can do except try to look after one's self and learn to laugh.

It's New Year's and I'm yearning for *azuki*-filled rice cakes.

I often dream of my monkey. I remember the way he used to sit on the windowsill with his head cocked to one side, watching the trams go by. He looked so cute. I really loved him, more than anyone will ever know. I wish he hadn't died. When I'm dead, I don't want to be buried with other people, I want to be buried beside my little Ah-fu.

I never imagined I would be going before you.

Take good care of yourself!

Yoshiko

There was still some blank space left on the paper, and she filled it with a cartoonish sketch of Ah-fu. She sealed the letter in an envelope and wrote the name of the recipient on the outside: *Mr. Naniwa Kawashima.*

She was beyond love or hate now and was letting everything go.

Later, the warden came shouting for her.

"There's someone here from the State Auditor's Council, and he wants to see you!"

Barely able to rouse herself, she protested listlessly, "They've already cleaned me out! Everything's been accounted for!"

But she dragged herself up, rubbed at the dirt around her eyes with the back of her hand, and hacked a foul cough. They had taken everything from her that they possibly could—her wealth, her future. What did they want from her now? Unwilling even to look up at her visitor, she heard him addressing her in official jargon:

"Our auditors came across a confiscated necklace. It's in the shape of a phoenix and is set with about a thousand diamonds of varying shapes and sizes. We weren't sure whether it was yours or not. We need your confirmation either way."

His voice was familiar. But so cold, so lacking in feeling. She jerked her head up to look at him, and her slack nerves snapped to attention. She was speechless. This unexpected guest, this official functionary in a tailored suit, was Yun Kai!

22

Not once, in all the intervening years, did she even dream she would meet Yun Kai again, least of all in such embarrassing circumstances.

"I'll be in the visiting room," he said with no trace of emotion.

He left her completely flustered. She felt so inferior, so old and ugly. She had lost her self-respect a long time ago—how could she face him? Her hands fluttered helplessly as she paced back and forth. What was she going to do?

Hastily running a comb through her hair, she found it stiff with dirt, so she rubbed in a little bit of peanut oil. There were no mirrors in prison, but she had fashioned a makeshift one out of a shard of broken glass and a piece of black paper. Scanning around the room, she seized on some tooth powder, which she used as a substitute for face powder, rubbing it onto her face until her skin was white. She found a piece of red paper on an old candy box and rubbed that against her lips in place of lipstick, blending the color with saliva. A glance in her makeshift mirror didn't give her much comfort, but what more could she do?

At length she decided she was ready to go to the visiting room. Taking a long, deep breath, she sought to compose herself.

The warden brought her, straight-backed and resolute, before Yun Kai. She was putting on an air of confidence so that he would not see how old and broken down she was, but the effort only made her feel worse.

Yun Kai looked uncomfortable. Struggling to hold herself erect, Yoshiko sat down opposite him. She spoke first, in a husky voice that surprised even herself.

"Would you mind telling me what you're doing here?"

Yun Kai picked up the necklace and meaningfully laid it on the table between them. Although it sparkled and danced with inner fires, that phoenix still could not fly.

"We hoped you could identify this for us and tell us whether or not it's yours. Once we've verified its origins, we can record it as confiscated property and dispose of it."

Yoshiko gave a rueful chuckle.

"Since it's been confiscated already, I can hardly claim that it belongs to me anymore, now can I?"

She folded her arms across her chest in an attempt to conceal her discomfort and her wildly pounding heart. He leaned toward her, and she looked at him in disbelief. What was he up to? A welter of suspicions crowded her mind.

"Are you absolutely positive?" he said, bending closer still.

Then, with a swift and nervous glance around him, he whispered in Yoshiko's ear.

"When you go before the firing squad, the bullets will be blanks, but no one there will know. When you hear the shots, you must pretend to be hit and collapse to the ground. I'll take it from there. I owe you a life, and I came to repay my debt."

Repay a debt? For a moment, she didn't know what he was talking about, but then she remembered. Years ago he stood in the sights of her gun—she could have killed him, but in the end she merely grazed his hair. She let him live. And now he sat before her, the only thing that stood between her and certain death. Experience taught her the importance of playing it cool when the stakes were high. She mustn't give anything away.

She heard him out; while they reached a silent understanding, her face remained immobile—but her eyes spoke volumes as she fixed him with a brief, penetrating gaze. She looked down at the necklace.

"Of course I'll cooperate with the government, but—" She hesitated, searching Yun Kai's face and stealing a brief glance at the guard standing just outside the room. "You have confiscated all of my personal property," she intoned loudly, as though making a public pronouncement. "Please allow me one final concession. I would like a kimono, made of white silk—in exchange for all of my worldly goods. Would that be possible, sir?"

Her eyes were filled with worried tears. There was nothing more she could say. Her heart pounded, and her stomach was tying itself in knots.

Yun Kai gave her hand a tight squeeze, squeezing so hard that his knuckles went white, and she felt the pain all the way to her heart. Neither of them spoke—a thousand words and a thousand feelings all came together in that one brief contact. In a moment, they would have to let go.

A bittersweet sensation washed over Yoshiko, and she had to fight back the tears. She couldn't allow herself to show any weakness.

Nodding officiously, he gathered up his things, giving her once last glance. Her lips trembled, and though no sound escaped them, he could read them clearly:

"Ah-fu!"

She dropped her head and went out. This time she wanted to be the first to leave. She never wanted to watch a man walk away from her again.

Did he mean what he said? She kept her doubts at bay. She had been disappointed before, but she wanted so much to believe in this last glimmer of hope. Nonetheless, she faced her future with equanimity. She was over forty years old, and the best years of her life were behind her. Her days of power and influence were but memories. All that awaited her was a slow decline and public humiliation. She had been a fighter, a commander—to die by the gun would be heroic, she told herself. What was more, all of her old associates were in the same situation. They were a politically ambitious crowd of Japanese officers, spies, and war criminals. All of them were guilty of something, and with the UN forces after them, it was only a matter of time before their pasts caught up with them. Why should she be any different?

She wondered sometimes if her trial hadn't been just a staged spectacle, the ending written before the action even started, her death sentence an inevitability. She had lost that round. Yun Kai's appearance would be the last round in this high-stakes game of chance. She was impatient for the players to show their hands. She wanted it over soon—the wait was excruciating.

* * *

It was still dark out. March 25, 1948, was about to dawn. Yoshiko's time had come, but no trace of fear clouded her expression, and no lines of worry furrowed her brow. Turning from the white silk kimono she was laying out, she saw the warden glowering down at her.

"I don't want to die in these prison rags—" she started to explain.

But he simply shook his head. She didn't protest—she knew she couldn't expect any special favors from him, so she might as well just do as he wished. Sighing with regret, she swept aside the soft, insubstantial garment.

A white silk kimono. She was only seven years old when she put on her first kimono. The memory was bittersweet. She cried and complained, trying with all her might to tear it off—it was like a straitjacket. She couldn't get it off, no matter how hard she fought, but she would learn to love it. On that day, they had remade her.

"I am Chinese!" she had cried. She really didn't want to be Japanese. Still, in the end, it was the Chinese who sentenced her to death. She was only seven years old.

"If you won't let me wear it, then so be it. I don't really care, anymore. There's plenty of honor in dying before a firing squad—it's a privilege, like attending a banquet. I'll just be a little underdressed, that's all."

Yoshiko turned again to the warden.

"May I write my will?"

He watched in silence as she hurriedly gathered up every last bank note she had.

"It's not even enough to buy a piece of paper," she sobbed, knowing that the big stack of bills she offered was practically worthless. But the warden handed her a blank scrap of paper.

With pen raised over the blank sheet, she hesitated for a moment, lost in thought.

"Hurry up!" the warden barked. "You're out of time!"

It was a just hazy recollection, the poem she was trying to remember. She had to hurry. It was too late. She was out of time. And then she remembered.

I have a home I can't return to,
I'm full of tears I cannot cry.
The only law here is injustice,
Who will listen to my story?

Carefully and reverently, Yoshiko folded the paper into four, so that it would fit into the palm of her hand.

"I'm sure China will be better off without me!" she said bitterly. "I've never wanted anything but the best for China—it's a shame I won't live to see it!"

The warden glanced at his watch, and Yoshiko knew it was time. There was no point in putting it off, even if she could. As much as she loved her life, she knew she couldn't cling to it forever. As these thoughts raced through her mind, an enigmatic smile that she alone understood formed on her lips—it was time for the dealer to show his hand.

She strode out of her cell, tall and undaunted. There was a chill in the air that made the prisoners shiver. A shudder ran through Yoshiko's body, but she remained composed. With her proud bearing, she looked more like an empress reviewing her troops than a convict about to be executed.

As the guards let her out, she became aware of someone humming a song. Sad and shrill, it sent a shiver down her spine.

The fairest flowers rarely bloom,
The finest days give way to clouds,
Sorrow fills the brightest smiles,
And teardrops mar the clearest skin.
After we part tonight,
Will we ever meet again?
Let's drain this glass
And have another round.
Let's laugh together while we can,
Who knows what tomorrow will bring?

Yoshiko sang along dreamily:

After we part tonight,
Will we ever meet again?

Tenderness and despair filled her heart. Oh, China, she mused, someday you will understand, someday you will feel as I do. She clutched the poem tightly in her fist.

In a dark corner of the prison, a white silk kimono lay discarded in a heap.

The people of Peking were still adrift in the sweetness of sleep as Yoshiko was led to the execution ground in the first pale light of dawn. She stood facing the wall while the executioner read out the sentence:

"Yoshiko Kawashima, born Princess Hsien-tzu, fourteenth daughter of the Manchu prince Su, sometimes known as Eastern Jewel, also known as Chin Pi-hui, forty-two years of age, has been convicted of the crime of treason. All appeals have been denied, and she has been sentenced to death, with the sentence to be carried out on this morning, the twenty-fifth day of March, 1948."

They made her kneel.

There was a sharp click as the executioner released the safety catch on his gun. Yoshiko moved almost imperceptibly, the piece of paper clutched tight in her hand.

A sudden flash of realization coursed through her body like an electric shock: She was standing on that narrow precipice between life and death, and she was afraid. No man or woman, no matter how brave, no matter how committed to a cause, could help but feel a jolt of apprehension before the barrel of the executioner's gun.

23

A shot rang out.

Outside the prison gates, a rumble of disapproval rose up from the throng of reporters who were gathered there to cover the story. They had just been cheated out of seeing this execution firsthand. Rumor originally had it that the execution was to take place at Municipal Prison Number Two on the previous day; at the last minute, the time and place were changed.

The press was out in full force this early morning. There was even a film crew from the Central Film Studio, hoping for footage for a documentary on Yoshiko's life. They were extremely disappointed that the final, and most dramatic, scene would be missing. Why had everything been so hastily arranged, they all wondered?

Everybody was in an uproar, but the soldiers standing guard didn't give an inch, answering every entreaty from the press with the same stern directive: Under no circumstances were the prison gates to be opened without the explicit permission of the head warden. Nor were they, the guards, permitted to answer any questions. Reporters crowded forward, thrusting their calling cards into the guards' faces, but they might as well have been dealing with a brick wall.

It was while the press was negotiating with the prison authorities that the muffled report of a gunshot reached their ears. At first they weren't sure what they had heard—had the execution been carried out in secret? What had happened?

Just then, day broke. As the first rays of sunlight fell upon the land, the people of Peking began another day, just like any other. But for the executed, this day was different—for her there would be no more dawns, no more tomorrows.

The warden was escorting a Japanese monk to the west gate of the prison, where a body lay atop a plain white casket. The body was that of a woman, her face covered by an old straw mat that was anchored in place with a couple of broken bricks—to keep the wind from blowing the straw mat off. The corpse was clothed in a gray prison uniform and blue cloth shoes. The monk, Master Furukawa, stepped forward to identify the body.

Yoshiko never knew Master Furukawa, although he was a prominent and highly regarded Buddhist monk, former abbot, and president of the North China Buddhist Federation. Many of his seventy-eight years had been spent roaming far and wide and spreading the faith. He had followed Yoshiko's case with great interest. He also knew that her friends, relatives, and other associates were reluctant to identify her body in public, lest the stain of her crimes contaminate them, as well. When none of them proved willing to step forward, Master Furukawa took the teachings of his Mahayana Buddhism to heart. Remembering that one should despise the crime but not the criminal, he petitioned the court for permission to verify the identity of the executed.

Stepping up to the coffin, he lifted the mat covering the face. The bullet had entered at the back of the head, emerging from the right side of the face. The shot was fired at close range, leaving the face an unrecognizable mass of blood and bone, with a purplish stain around the entry wound.

Furukawa mumbled a sutra as he wiped away some of the blood with a cotton rag; but it was still impossible to tell what the face had looked like in life. A clutch of reporters rushed up while he was wrapping the body in a white wool blanket. They busily snapped pictures in a flurry of shouting as they jostled for a better view. After all, she was a legend.

Everybody was talking at once.

"Was she shot?"

"What's the point of just getting a picture of the body?"

"All that detailed groundwork—for this?"

"How did you find out about it? Who told you?"

"Is it really Yoshiko Kawashima?"

"I can't tell! The face is a bloody mess—I can't make out a damn thing!"

"Don't you think there's something strange about the way they handled this—not letting us reporters in to see the execution?"

"I thought she had short hair. How come the hair on this corpse is so long?"

"Maybe it isn't really Yoshiko."

In the midst of this hubbub, Master Furukawa calmly continued to wrap the body, first in a fresh blanket and last in a multicolored quilt—a fitting end to a colorful life. He droned on, chanting funeral sutras, his robes stained with blood, while a pair of young acolytes helped carry the body to a waiting truck, right past the disgruntled band of journalists. The journalists remained rooted to the spot, their discussion raging long after the truck had left for the crematorium. Meanwhile, an urgent call reached the newspaper office, demanding an investigation, but the body was long gone.

When the truck reached the crematorium, the monks and the crematorium employees moved the body into a room. They did so without reverence or ceremony—it was a just a job to them. They saw death every day. They didn't care whose body it was. As far as they were concerned, a corpse was a corpse, incapable of feeling, incapable of breathing—just plain dead. Rich or poor, high or low, good or bad, beautiful or ugly—they were all the same here. All were destined to be turned to ash in a moment's time.

As the corpse was carried in, one of its hands fell limply out, and a slip of paper fluttered to the floor. But nobody noticed. Nobody ever knew.

The monks read a final blessing, the kindling was readied, and the men withdrew. Several hours later, the roaring flames had transformed the entire body to ash. The cremation was complete by one-thirty in the afternoon. Master Furukawa and his attendants took the ashes and divided them. Half would be sent to Mr. Kawashima to enshrine; the other half would be given a proper burial in the crematorium graveyard.

As the monks interred the box of ashes, they gave Yoshiko a Buddhist name—Sister Aisin of the Blue Moss and Wondrous

Fragrance. She was nobody's wife, none of her family would acknowledge her, and her foster father was in another country— so the monks settled for "Sister." A large crowd gathered around to watch the ceremony, but none of them had come to mourn. The only mourners were the monks, a handful of strangers burning offerings of incense for her in the chill wind. This was how Sister Aisin of the Blue Moss and Wondrous Fragrance left the world. Born in 1907. Died in 1948. A life.

Epilogue

The caller who demanded an inquiry refused to give up, and soon the Attorney General's Office received a letter of complaint. The dead woman was not Yoshiko Kawashima, it claimed, but rather the writer's sister, Liu Feng-ling! The matter was blown wide open, and indignant public opinion spread quickly to the courts. According to the complainant, one Liu Feng-chen, the "truth" was this:

> Her sister, Liu Feng-ling, bore a close resemblance to Yo-shiko Kawashima and had also been sentenced to death. Furthermore, Feng-ling happened to be seriously ill. When someone came from the prison and offered to give the

family ten gold ingots if they would let her be executed as a stand-in, the family (namely the mother and husband of the condemned) accepted. But after the execution, they only received four ingots; when they tried to get the rest of their gold, the people they had made the deal with had them thrown out. Then the mother went to demand an explanation—and she disappeared!

There was a great public outcry, with the newspapers printing one sensational story after another and the authorities ordering an official inquiry. The controversy raged for several months, with no sign of abating, as everyone wondered: Is Yoshiko Kawashima still alive? The investigation got under way, accompanied by bold headlines in all the dailies. But the complainant didn't give a complete address, nor did she name the parties she accused of making the trade. The inquiry stalled. Meanwhile, the elderly monk, Furukawa, testified in court that the body was indeed Yoshiko's, and not that of a stand-in. But the issue was by no means settled.

Some time afterward, Master Furukawa went back to Japan, arriving at Kawashima's lakeside lodge in the mountains of Honshu with an urn tucked under his arm. The seventy-eight-year-old monk was greeted by the eighty-five-year-old Kawashima. Together, the two frail old men went out to bury Yoshiko's ashes. They placed several articles she once used in the ground along with the urn: an old velvet coverlet, a hot-water bottle, and a white kimono.

"Even if it isn't Yoshiko," Kawashima offered, "don't you suppose we'd better say a blessing over her just in case?"

To this day, the mystery surrounding the details of her death has remained unsolved.

* * *

Nine months after receiving Yoshiko's ashes, Naniwa Kawashima was having his temperature taken by the nurse who visited him every day at dusk. She had just inserted the thermometer under his armpit when she noticed he had stopped breathing. Never again would he see the sky filled with snowflakes. The exuberant camaraderie of his youth was but a distant echo. He hadn't even lasted until nightfall.

His tombstone, bearing the Buddhist name of Grand Hermit of Sokutsufugai, Shosoin Monastery, sits in a silent row with those of his dead wife, Fukuko, and his foster daughter, Yoshiko, in the Kawashima family plot.

That year saw the execution of vast numbers of war criminals in Peking. Loaded onto the backs of trucks, their hands tied behind their backs, the condemned were paraded around the city on their way to the execution ground. Large characters painted on the sides of the trucks announced their crimes: murder and mayhem, abuse of power, extortion, and other atrocities. The crowds of spectators lining the roads became inflamed and started hurling bricks at the prisoners in the trucks, shouting out epithets all the while:

"Death to the Eastern devils!"

"An eye for an eye!"

"Death is too good for them!"

Many of the condemned were dead by the time they reached the execution ground, but some of them still clung to life. They awaited death, punished to the last by the pain of their broken bodies. Among them was Shunkichi Uno. His death was even more miserable than Yoshiko's.

China's people would never forget the harsh lessons of history.

* * *

Disillusioned by the corruption and ineffectiveness of the Nationalist government, Yun Kai made his way to Yen'an, where he joined the Communists. There he was neither Yun Kai nor Ah-fu, and what he did with the rest of his life remains a mystery.

Pu-yi, the "emperor" of Manchukuo, was apprehended in 1946 by the Soviet Red Army at the Shenyang airport as he tried to flee. They brought him to the International Military Tribunal in Tokyo, where he was tried. Later, while serving out his sentence at a reeducation camp in the Northeast of China, he wrote an account of his life.

Yamaga, who had defied his top-secret orders to assassinate Yoshiko, was detained the moment he reported to headquarters. After his interrogation, he was imprisoned for a time. He lay low until the end of the war, afraid to show his face lest he be branded a war criminal and shipped back to China to stand trial. The dignified gentleman who once strolled around elegantly in a Chinese scholar's robes, wearing a felt hat, carrying a staff, and speaking perfect Mandarin, was now just a down-and-out Japanese debtor, with creditors at his heels.

In January of 1950, the *Morning Sun Weekly* featured the following lead story:

A wild dog was found gnawing on the head of a man in the slops of a pigsty! Several spots on the skull still bore traces of hair, but the face and neck had already been chewed down to the bone. This was big news in the tiny town of Hsishan in Shanli county, and the locals hastily mounted a search for the rest of the body. It was finally discovered in a grove of pines, a headless corpse bound to a tree trunk with hemp rope. Beside the body was a black satchel containing some sleeping pills, a few papers, and six letters. . . .

It was Yamaga, dead at fifty-three. He didn't believe the fortune-teller:

"Born in 1894 . . . noble in appearance. In ten years he will die miserably because of a woman. He will commit suicide, his body left in the wilderness to be eaten by wild dogs."

The medium instructed him:

". . . if he can avoid this disaster, his luck will change and he will know untold riches."

Fate worked in mysterious ways, inexorably. In the end, the fortune came true, but did it have to be that way? Did he have to die, all because of one woman? And what really happened to her? Was she dead or alive?

Time is like a river, flowing ever on, leaving us behind on the shore. And when we are gone, all that remains of us are shadows dancing on the wind. Our successes and failures, our victories and defeats, truths and falsehoods, loves and hates—in the end, they are all the same. China's three thousand years of history has been one long tale of death and destruction—year after year, century after century, flowers have turned to dust, white bones have turned to ash. But the river flows on, and the red leaves of autumn dance in the wind and come fluttering down.

Years passed. There was civil war in China, followed by more internal strife. Chinese people ruthlessly attacked each other for the real and imagined sins of the past. The blood never stopped flowing.

Japan lost the war and knew the humiliation of rebuilding a nation from the ground up; but in the end Japan became rich and powerful, the envy of the world.

Afterword

The busiest and most lively part of Tokyo is the Ginza. A forest of skyscrapers, a commercial and financial center, it is also home to a bevy of famous apartment stores: Mitsukoshi, Matsuzaka-ya, Seibu, and Tokyu, to name just a few.

On Sundays, a few of the streets in this bustling district are blocked off, and the area becomes a "strollers' paradise" where a holiday atmosphere prevails. It is always packed with prosperous shoppers in high spirits, all of them wandering around and having a good time eating, drinking, shopping, or just taking in the scene.

Sometimes you might catch a glimpse of the retreating figure of an old woman. She wears a white kimono, and a little monkey perches on her shoulder. Dignified, but a bit forlorn, she is gone in the blink of an eye, swallowed up in the sea of weekenders, gone without a trace.

Who is she? you might ask yourself. You didn't get a very good look at her. Maybe it was just your imagination, a ghost of the distant past.